THE ELSON READERS—BOOK FOUR
A Teacher's Guide

———◆———

Catherine Andrews

B.A. English Education, National Board Certified, Teacher of English, International Baccalaureate/Bartow High School

Mary Jane Newcomer

B.A. English Education, Teacher of English, Frostproof Middle-Senior High School, Frostproof, Florida

Lost Classics
Book Company
Lake Wales, Florida

PUBLISHER'S NOTE

Recognizing the need to return to more traditional principles in education, Lost Classics Book Company is republishing forgotten late 19th and early 20th century literature and textbooks to aid parents in the education of their children.

This guide is designed to accompany *The Elson Readers—Book Four,* which was reprinted from the 1920 copyright edition. This guide contains all the original questions and exercises from the reader along with suggested answers. It also includes new study sections for stories included in the original reader that were not addressed in the "Helps to Study."

We have included the same glossary and pronunciation guide of more than 900 terms at the end of the book that is included in the reader, and which has been updated with pronunciation notation currently in use.

The Elson Readers—Book Four, which this volume is meant to accompany, has been assigned a reading level of 960L. More information concerning this reading level assessment may be attained by visiting www.lexile.com.

© Copyright 2005
Lost Classics Book Company
ISBN 978-1-890623-28-9
Designed to Accompany
The Elson Readers—Book Four
ISBN 978-1-890623-18-0
Part of
The Elson Readers
Nine Volumes: *Primer* through *Book Eight*
ISBN 978-1-890623-23-4

On the Cover:
Tiger Lily, from *Through the Looking Glass* (litho)
Tenniel, Sir John (1820-1914)
Private Collection/Bridgeman Art Library

TABLE OF CONTENTS

** *The first number refers to the page in the reader on which the story begins; the second refers to the page in the "Helps to Study" section in the back of the student's reader where the pertinent questions appear.*

PART IV: FAMOUS HEROES OF LONG AGO

PART V: GREAT AMERICAN AUTHORS

A NOTE ABOUT THIS GUIDE

Teachers and students alike may notice a difference in punctuation, capitalization, and spelling between the prose and poetry sections in the reader. Rules for these matters have changed since the original reader's publication, and we have decided that in the prose sections it would be in the best interest of the student to update these items so they will learn these rules as practiced today. However, the stories remain completely unabridged. We have exercised constraint, and typical changes consist of, for example: commas used in place of semicolons when appropriate, lowercase treatment of words not personified, or hyphenated spelling of words being contracted to modern spellings. We have, however, followed the traditional editorial practice of not changing these items in works of poetry, leaving these matters to the prerogative of the poet.

The reader was originally published just after World War One and many discussion questions refer to this great event. These questions can often be used to start discussion on that war and conflicts that occured after it. See the "Appendix" for a brief description of this war.

Language is always changing and when the student notices these changes it is often a good place to start a discussion on topics such as: personification, comma usage, "up" or "down" style of capitalization, etc.

Student worksheets do not inlude those exercises designed as group activities, which may result in non-sequential numbering of questions on those pages.

We have used *The Chicago Manual of Style*, 14th Edition, published by the University of Chicago, as our primary reference for these changes.

THE ELSON READERS—BOOK FOUR
A TEACHER'S GUIDE

HOW TO USE THIS BOOK

This *Teacher's Guide* was developed to provide teachers with a guideline for appropriate grade-level student responses to the questions found in the "Helps to Study" section of the reader. Some extended activities have been added to those discussion questions in this manual and may be used at the teacher's discretion to reinforce comprehension and appreciation of the work in question. Unfamiliar vocabulary terms have also been added at the end of each discussion guide in the *Teacher's Guide* to encourage students to broaden their use of language.

In addition to responses for existing study helps, discussion questions and activities have been created for those stories and poems in the reader for which there were no helps originally. Those questions and accompanying activities, found in this manual, were designed to develop the same basic comprehension and higher order thinking skills as those found in the reader.

Teachers may wish to have students begin with "Part One" and read the book in order, or they may pick and choose the works that fit their classroom goals. The parts are not sequential; however, skills introduced in one part may be reinforced in later parts allowing students to practice and master the various literary skills as outlined in the objectives found at the beginning of each part in the *Teacher's Guide*.

These questions and activities were designed to give the students a greater understanding of the world around them and a deeper appreciation for the contributions of those who have helped to build that world. In addition, students will receive instruction in the qualities so essential to their development as future productive citizens in the world they will inherit.

Suggestions for Silent Reading

Stories marked with a † lend themselves well to silent reading exercise.

(a) Have the students read the story silently as rapidly as they can, to get the main idea. Reading with the lips or pointing with the fingers slows speed. Encourage them to try steadily to increase their speed in silent reading.

(b) Let the students test themselves by: 1. seeing how many of the questions they can answer after one reading and 2. telling the main thoughts of the story. They may have to read the story again to be able to answer all the questions and to tell the story completely.

PART I:
OUR COUNTRY AND OUR HOMES

In This Section—

These stories and poems do not have "Helps to Study" questions in the reader. However, questions have been added in this teacher's guide to address those selections. These additional questions appear on separate worksheets which may be copied for the students.

**The first number refers to the page in the reader on which the story begins; the second refers to the page in the "Helps to Study" section in the back of the student's reader where the pertinent questions appear.*

7

Objectives—

By completing "Part I" the following objectives will be met:

    1. The student will use effective reading strategies to construct meaning and identify purpose of text including:
        a. using illustrations
        b. defining unfamiliar words
        c. retelling and summarizing

    2. The student will determine the main idea or essential message and identify relevant supporting details and facts of a text.

    3. The student will read and organize facts from the text and other sources to make a report and outline and perform an authentic task.

    4. The student will prepare for writing by focusing on the topic and organizing supporting details in a logical sequence.

    5. The student will draft and revise writing in cursive.

    6. The student will produce final documents that have been edited for correct spelling and punctuation.

    7. The student will write for a variety of audiences and purposes.

    8. The student will write in a variety of genres including narration, exposition, and poetry.

    9. The student will use speaking strategies effectively such as using eye contact and gestures that engage the audience.

10. The student will be familiar with the common features of fiction and nonfiction.

11. The student will identify the development of plot and how conflicts are resolved in a story.

12. The student will identify and understand similarities and differences among the characters, settings, and events presented in various texts.

13. The student will identify and use literary terminology such as rhyme scheme and personification.

14. The student will respond critically to fiction, nonfiction, poetry, and drama.

15. The student will recognize cause-and-effect relationships in literary texts.

16. The student will respond to a text by explaining how the motives of the characters or events compare with those in his or her own life.

17. The student will understand the qualities necessary for people to become good citizens and apply those qualities to his/her personal life.

18. The student will understand the qualities necessary to develop good character.

YOUR BOOK-COMRADE, p. 11

1. **What can your book-comrade do for you that your school-comrades cannot do?**

   Your book-comrade can "tell you stories of exciting things that have happened all over the world, all sorts of people and animals and fairies and all sorts of times."

2. **Can you name the five kinds of things your book-comrade promises to show you?**

   There are five things your book-comrade promises to show you:
   a. glimpses of things that make us love our country
   b. the fairy-land of adventure where you'll meet funny people and funnier animals
   c. the wonderland of nature
   d. far off lands across the sea into a time that has passed
   e. famous American authors

3. **What will you gain if you make friends of books?**

   If you make friends of books, "every year of your life will be made happier, wiser, and richer."

Extended Activities:

1. A web is a graphic organizer that helps students to visualize how a variety of ideas connect to a topic. Webs can be simple or complex. Webs provide the learner with opportunities to recall prior knowledge and identify patterns of information. Students should write the topic in the center circle, then list answers to the questions in the margins provided.

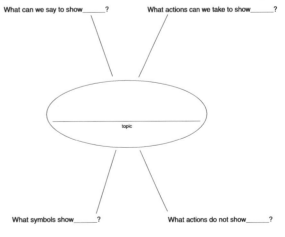

Have students make a web of patriotism or citizenship. (You may copy the diagram on page 10 in the *Teacher's Guide* for students.)

2. A collage is a picture that contains a wide array of images centered on a single topic. The pictures can overlap or be arranged symmetrically. Have students make a collage of America by using pictures from magazines.

3. A diorama is a three dimensional illustration. Have students make a diorama of their favorite book.

YOUR BOOK-COMRADE, P. 11

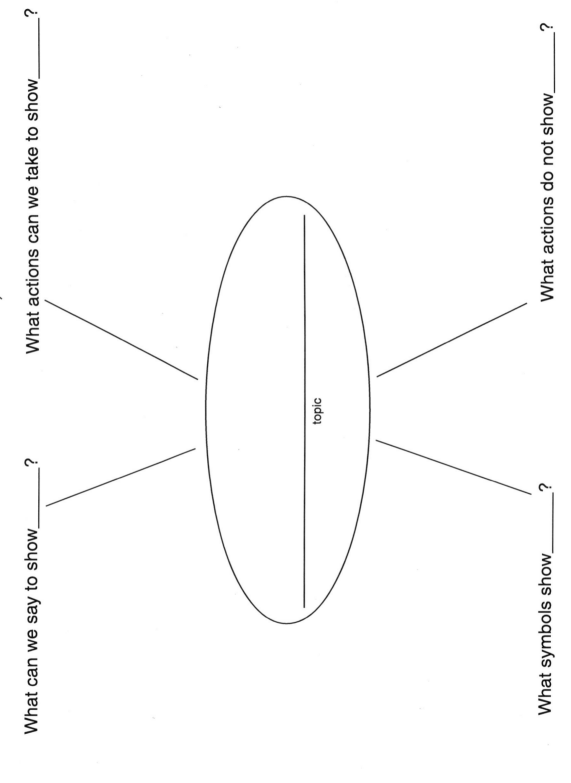

What can we say to show ____?

What actions can we take to show ____?

topic

What actions do not show ____?

What symbols show ____?

Lord Cornwallis's Knee-Buckles, p. 17

1. **In the Revolutionary War the American Colonies fought for freedom from Great Britain; on which side were Anne's father and brothers?**

   Anne's father and brothers were on the American side, joining the army under the command of George Washington.

2. **What good qualities did Anne show?**

   Anne showed many good qualities. Answers will vary, but may include: courtesy towards her elders, bravery for going to speak to General Cornwallis, and loyalty for being a good friend to her animal.

3. **What good qualities did Cornwallis show?**

   General Cornwallis also showed many good qualities. Answers will vary but may include: courtesy to speak with a young girl and generosity for returning Anne's cow.

4. **Why was Anne called a "rebel"?**

   Rebels are "people who are setting up a government of their own, and fighting those who ruled them before." Anne was called a rebel because her father and brothers were rebels, fighting for the Americans.

5. **Why did she think that her cow must be a "rebel cow"?**

   Anne thought her cow must be a rebel cow since she was a rebel.

6. **Why do you think Anne would become a good American citizen?**

   Anne would make a good citizen because she was loyal to her country and her home.

7. **Read aloud, with the help of one of your classmates, the conversation between Anne and the general.**

8. *Contest:* **which team of two can score highest in making this dialogue sound real?**

Find in the glossary the meaning of: quarters, rebels.
Find in the glossary the pronunciation of: Cornwallis.

A GLIMPSE OF WASHINGTON, p. 21

1. **Why did not the corporal help the soldiers?**
   The corporal did not help the soldiers because he thought he was better than they.

2. **In the "Forward Look," page 15, your book-comrade said that you would "chuckle a bit" at what you would hear General Washington saying; what did Washington say to the corporal that made you laugh?**
   The words of General Washington that possibly would make you laugh are when he tells the corporal sarcastically that he was the general and adds, "the next time you have a log too heavy for your men to lift, send for me."

3. **How did Washington show that he was ready to help his men?**
   General Washington showed he was ready to help his men because he did what they did. He did not consider himself above doing what he would ask his men to do.

4. **Dramatize the story.**
   A rubric is a holistic evaluation. In creating a rubric the evaluator decides what qualities of the product, process, and/or performance needs to be effectively evident. For the rubric given below the teacher will rate the student on a scale of poor to excellent on five aspects of his/her performance. The teacher can also assign a point value if he/she desires.
   Evaluation Rubric:

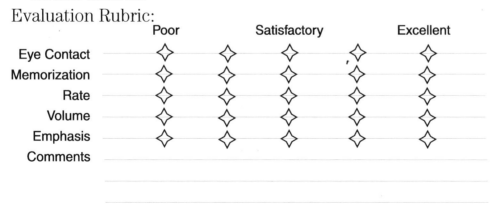

Find in the glossary the meaning of: corporal, fortified, breastwork.

A GLIMPSE OF WASHINGTON, p. 21

	Poor		Satisfactory		Excellent
Eye Contact	✧	✧	✧	✧	✧
Memorization	✧	✧	✧	✧	✧
Rate	✧	✧	✧	✧	✧
Volume	✧	✧	✧	✧	✧
Emphasis	✧	✧	✧	✧	✧
Comments					

	Poor		Satisfactory		Excellent
Eye Contact	✧	✧	✧	✧	✧
Memorization	✧	✧	✧	✧	✧
Rate	✧	✧	✧	✧	✧
Volume	✧	✧	✧	✧	✧
Emphasis	✧	✧	✧	✧	✧
Comments					

A SONG FOR FLAG DAY, p. 23

1. **Can you tell where our flag flies over our land, yet "half a world away"?**

   Our flag flies over our land, yet "half a world away" because our country is so large. The United States consists of the continental United States which includes Alaska located north of Canada. The distance from the southern part of Florida to the northern part of Alaska is almost "half a world away." In addition, Hawaii is a state belonging to the Union as well. From the east coast of the continental United States to Hawaii is a "half a world away." Our flag also flies at our embassies in countries around the world.

2. **The poet suggests that our "forefathers" who first settled in America "dreamed" that this country would always stand for bravery, truth, and justice. How did our fighting in World War I prove that their dream was true?**

   The poet suggests that our "forefathers," who first settled America, "dreamed" that this country would always stand for bravery, truth and justice. Our fighting in World War I proved that their dream was true because we were brave to fight the war and we fought for truth and justice.

3. **Which is the better way to help our country, to honor the flag with "glad salutes," or prove ourselves good citizens by being thrifty, working faithfully, and being kind to our neighbors?**

   The better way to help our country is to prove ourselves good citizens by being thrifty, working faithfully, and being kind to our neighbors. These actions help our country more than honoring our flag with "glad salutes."

4. **Memorize these two stanzas.**

Find in the glossary the meaning of: guidon.

A Story of the Flag, p. 24

1. **Why is the flag of the United States better known in France today than it was before World War I?**

    The flag of the United States is better known in France today than it was before World War I because we helped France during the war and were allies with her.

2. **What new idea came to Frank at the sight of the American flag in Paris?**

    The new idea that came to Frank at the sight of the American flag in Paris was "that the United States was one of a great many nations living next to one another in this world—and that his own nation was kind of a big family to which he belonged."

3. **Why did the Consul place an American flag on the Frenchman's tomb?**

    The Consul placed an American flag on the Frenchman's tomb because Lafayette helped the United States in the Revolutionary War.

4. **State in your own words the thought in the last sentence of this story.**

    Answers will vary but should contain the fact that the American flag is a symbol of liberty and justice.

Find in the glossary the meaning of: franc, consul, Lafayette, respect, justice.

Find in the glossary the pronunciation of: revolutionary.

Extended Activities:

Have students research one or more of the following topics in the encyclopedia and write a paragraph on what they learned: Betsy Ross, the American flag or Marquis de Lafayette. Have students plan their writing by organizing their information using the diagram at right. Students should write a draft, revise and edit, then write a final copy of their paragraph in cursive.

Topic	
	1
	2
	3
	4
5	
6	
7	
8	

A STORY OF THE FLAG, p. 24

Research one or more of the following topics in the encyclopedia and write a paragraph on what you learned: Betsy Ross, the American flag, or Marquis de Lafayette. Plan their writing by organizing your information using the diagram at right. You should write a draft, revise and edit, then write a final copy of your paragraph in cursive.

```
┌─────────────────┬──────────────────────┐
│                 │  1                   │
│                 ├──────────────────────┤
│                 │  2                   │
│                 ├──────────────────────┤
│                 │  3                   │
│                 ├──────────────────────┤
│                 │  4                   │
├─────────────────┴──────────────────────┤
│  5                                      │
├─────────────────────────────────────────┤
│  6                                      │
├─────────────────────────────────────────┤
│  7                                      │
├─────────────────────────────────────────┤
│  8                                      │
└─────────────────────────────────────────┘
```

_____

_____

_____

_____

_____

_____

_____

_____

_____

SOME GLIMPSES OF LINCOLN, P. 27

1. **Why was Lincoln chosen as umpire in the quarrel between the two boys?**

   Lincoln was chosen as umpire in the quarrel between the two boys because of his strong love for fair play.

2. **What quality did he show when the little bully offered to fight him?**

   The quality Lincoln showed when the little bully offered to fight him was fairness.

3. **What quality did he show in the case of the woodchopper? Have you read other stories of Lincoln that show any of these good qualities?**

   The quality Lincoln showed in the case of the woodchopper was kindness. Other reading suggestions: *Elson Reader— Book Two*, "Lincoln and His Dog" and *Elson Reader—Book Five*, "The Boyhood of Lincoln."

4. **Which of the qualities shown in these glimpses of Lincoln would help him to become a good leader for the United States?**

   The qualities Lincoln showed in these glimpses into his life that would make him a good leader for the United States were his eagerness for fairness and equality. He would be able to represent all people.

5. **In the "Forward Look," page 15, you read that you would "chuckle a bit" at what you hear Lincoln saying; what words of Lincoln in this story made you laugh?**

   The words in this story that might make one laugh is when Lincoln told the bully, "You are so small that there isn't much of you for me to hit, but I am so big that you can't help hitting me. So you make a chalk mark on me that will show just your size. When we fight, you must hit me inside this mark."

Find in the glossary the meaning of: dispute.

HOW THEODORE ROOSEVELT OVERCAME HIS HANDICAP, P. 29

1. **In what ways did Roosevelt try to make his body strong?**

   To make his body strong, Roosevelt took boxing lessons, wrestled and worked in a gym his dad built for him.

2. **How did pluck and perseverance aid him?**

   Pluck and perseverance aided Roosevelt by giving him the motivation and endurance to continue to help make his body strong.

3. **What rules for health does this story suggest?**

   This story suggests that we must exercise to have healthy bodies.

4. **How did he overcome his handicap?**

   Roosevelt overcame his handicap by working hard to build his muscles.

5. **How did Lincoln's handicap differ from Roosevelt's?**

   Roosevelt's handicap was different than Lincoln's. Roosevelt had a weak body (he suffered from acute asthma) but was able to strengthen his mind through formal education. Lincoln had a strong body but had little opportunity for formal education.

6. **What sentence on page 31 is illustrated by the picture on page 30 (above)?**

   The sentence on page 31 that is illustrated by the picture on page 30 is "Each day, he spent hours and hours in the saddle, rounding up the cattle with other cowboys."

7. **This story has three parts; the first ends with the second line on page 30; the second ends with the first paragraph on page 31; and the third completes the story; give a suitable title to each of the three parts.**
   Answers will vary.   1. Roosevelt's handicap   2. Roosevelt overcomes his handicap 3. Handicaps can be overcome.

8. **Listen while the story is read aloud by three good readers (one for each part).**

9. **How does this story encourage boys and girls who have some handicap in life?**
   This story encourages boys and girls with handicaps to use pluck and perseverance to strengthen their weaknesses.

Find in the glossary the meaning of: perseverance, poverty, stalwart.

Extended Activity:

Have students list five ways they can strengthen their bodies and minds.

Body	Mind

HOW THEODORE ROOSEVELT OVERCAME HIS HANDICAP, P. 29

List five ways you can strengthen your body and mind.

Body	Mind

A LITTLE SOLDIER OF THE AIR, p. 32

1. **This is a true story of World War I; what did homing pigeons do to help win the War?**

   Homing pigeons helped win the war by making "long, tiresome flights to carry messages for America and her allies."

2. **Why is "little soldiers of the air" a good name for these pigeons?**

   "Little soldiers of the air" is a good name for these pigeons because they were small creatures who flew in the air for the soldiers fighting for America.

3. **How did they carry their messages? Read aloud the paragraph that tells you.**

   The paragraph that tells you how the pigeons carried their messages is on page 32, the third paragraph, and continues to page 33.

4. **Tell the story of Cher Ami's service in saving the lives of some American soldiers.**

   The story of Cher Ami's service in saving the lives of some American soldiers can be summarized as follows: One October day the 77th Division was ordered to enemy lines. Some of the men, about 480, were ahead of the rest of the Division. They climbed up a hill where they stayed for the night. In the morning, they were surrounded by German soldiers. They tried to send pigeons to the American soldiers with messages for help. Each pigeon sent up was killed. Since soldiers were unable to break through enemy lines, Cher Ami was their last hope. When the little bird was released he was shot in the foot, but kept on flying. He was able to reach the home coop with the message. The soldiers were saved.

5. **What does the picture on page 32 (right) suggest to you? The picture on page 35 (previous page)?**

   The picture on page 32 suggests that the men valued and took care of the pigeons, and the picture on page 35 suggests that the men depended on the pigeon to help them. One can observe the look of hope in their faces.

6. **At what point in the story was your interest greatest?**

   Answers will vary. The climax of the story occurs when Cher Ami is released and the guns shot at him.

7. **Listen while the story of Cher Ami's service is read aloud by two good readers; the first will begin with the second paragraph on page 33, and read to the picture on page 35; the second will read the rest of the story.**

8. **It was the pigeon's love of home that led him to do this service for America; what led the American soldiers to go overseas to fight in World War I?**

   It was also the American soldiers' love of home that led them to fight in the war. They wanted to protect their homes and the values of the American people.

9. **Why should we feel proud of the soldiers who were saved by Cher Ami?**

   We should be proud of the soldiers who were saved by Cher Ami because they were in a bad situation, but they were brave and showed perseverance.

Find in the glossary the meaning of: Cher Ami.

THE QUEST, p. 37

1. **What did the restless boy learn as he traveled?**
    The boy saw fair lands and costly homes, but he learned that he was not contented in these places.

2. **What do you think he "missed" in the homes he saw that made him return to "the little brown house"?**
    The boy missed the familiarity he had with the "little brown house" and the area around it.

3. **One who really loves his home will help to make it a better place in which to live; in what ways do you help at home?**
    Answers will vary.

4. **Read aloud the lines on page 16 that tell what will make you a good citizen.**
    "Your love of home, and your faithfulness to the simple duties that make home worthwhile are the very things that will make you a good citizen."

5. **Mention some simple duties we owe to others in the home.**
    Students should answer such things as completing chores assigned to them, helping other family members and showing consideration to them.

6. **Why do you think one who loves his home will also love his country?**
    One who loves his home will also love his country, because home is a small part that makes up the country.

7. **Why is this poem a good one to read just after you have read "A Little Soldier of the Air"?**
    "The Quest" is a good poem to read after reading the story of Cher Ami because both demonstrate the same theme: love of home.

Find in the glossary the meaning of: content.

LITTLE BROWN HANDS, p. 38

1. **What does the first stanza tell us that the little brown hands will do? The second stanza? The third?**

   The first stanza tells us that little brown hands "drive home cows from the pasture." The second stanza tells us that little brown hands hoe hay and pick fruit. The third stanza tells us that little brown hands build castles on the beach, pick up seashells, and find bark that has drifted to land.

2. **What does the poet say that the owners of the "little brown hands" will do when they become men and women?**

   When the owners of the "little brown hands" become men and women, they will be "mighty rulers of state" or authors or artists.

3. **Can you name a man, of whom you have read in this book, who was "humble and poor" and became a "mighty ruler of state," that is, a strong head of a great nation?**

   Abraham Lincoln was a man who was "humble and poor" and became a "mighty ruler of state."

4. **Why is it true that "those who toil bravely are strongest"?**

   It is true that "those who toil bravely are strongest" because hard work produces strength.

5. **Explain the meaning of the last four lines of the poem, finding in the glossary the meaning of "statesman," "chisel," and "palette."**

   A statesman is a "man skilled in the affairs of government." A chisel is "a sharp iron tool used in carving statues and figures." A palette is "a plate on which a painter mixes his colors." The last four lines mean that the "little brown hands" will write great books and documents, fight bravely, and use the chisel and palette to make great works of art.

Find in the glossary the meaning of: elderbloom, delicate, toil, humble.

Extended Activities:

1. Have students draw a picture of their hand. In each finger students will write one thing they would like to do when they grow up.

2. Everyone has someone they admire. Have students choose someone whom they admire and write a paragraph explaining why they admire that person. What qualities does this person possess that help him/her to be a good citizen? Students may use the diagram below to help them plan their writing.

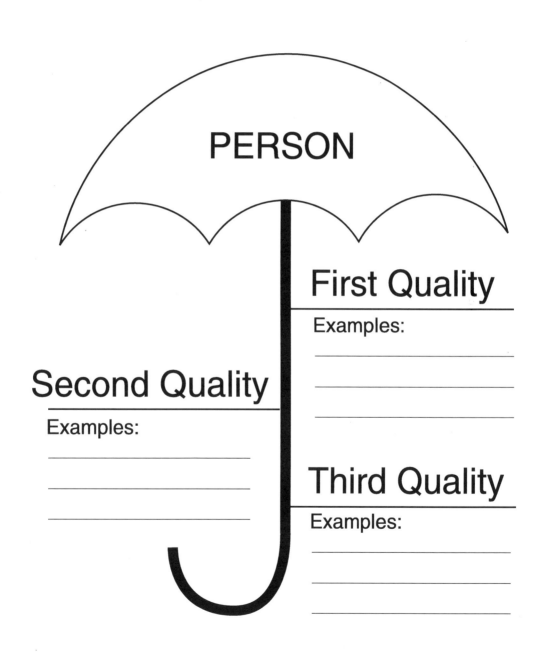

LITTLE BROWN HANDS, P. 38

1. Draw a picture of your hand. In each finger write one thing you would like to do when you grow up.

2. Everyone has someone they admire. Choose someone whom you admire and write a paragraph explaining why you admire that person. What qualities does this person possess that help him/her to be a good citizen? You may use the diagram to help you plan your writing.

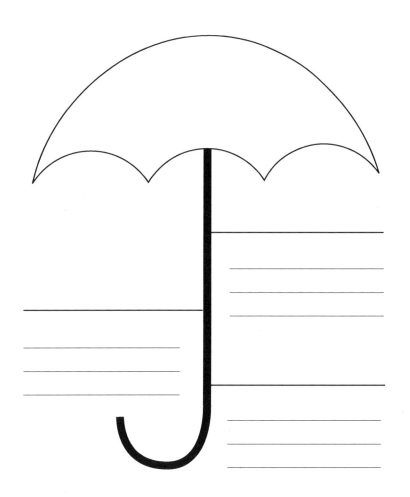

EVENING AT THE FARM,

p. **40***

1. **In the first stanza, what line lets the reader know it is evening?**

"His shadow lengthens along the land."

2. **What stanza does the picture on page 40 (above) illustrate?**

The picture illustrates the first stanza.

3. **What is the milkmaid doing in the second stanza?**

The milkmaid is milking her cows.

4. **What qualities do the farm-boy, the milkmaid, the farmer, and the farmer's wife all have in common?**

They all work hard and are faithful to their duties.

5. **Draw a picture of your favorite stanza.**

Find in the glossary the meaning of: mink; lowing; milch; heifer; tranquil; drowsily; repose; co', boss.

Extended Activity:

Have students go outside and draw their shadow with sidewalk chalk in the morning, the afternoon, and the evening. Have them observe how the size and position of their shadow changes. Have students write to explain their conclusions.

*This selection does not have "Helps to Study" questions in the reader.

Evening at the Farm, p. 40

1. In the first stanza, what line lets the reader know it is evening?

_____

_____

_____

2. What stanza does the picture on page 40 illustrate?

_____

_____

_____

3. What is the milkmaid doing in the second stanza?

_____

_____

_____

4. What qualities do the farm-boy, the milkmaid, the farmer, and the farmer's wife all have in common?

_____

_____

_____

5. Draw a picture of your favorite stanza in the space below.

Go outside and draw your shadow with sidewalk chalk in the morning, the afternoon, and the evening. Observe how the size and position of your shadow changes. Write to explain your conclusions.

_____

_____

_____

_____

_____

_____

_____

_____

_____

_____

_____

_____

_____

_____

_____

_____

_____

_____

_____

_____

_____

_____

_____

A Dog of Flanders, p. 42

1. Notice that this story has four parts, each with a title printed in smaller type than is used for the title of the story; they are called subtitles. Read the four subtitles. In "How Theodore Roosevelt Overcame His Handicap" you made subtitles for the story, while here they are made for you.

2. Tell the story, with the help of three of your classmates, using the subtitles as an outline, each telling one part.

3. The old man was kind; give instances of his kindness to the boy; the dog.

    The old man was kind to the boy by taking care of him when his mom died even though he was very old and poor. The old man was kind to the dog by nursing him back to health with his "tender touch" and "kindly word."

4. How were the old man and the little boy able to be happy, even though they were "terribly poor"?

    The old man and the little boy were able to be happy even though they were "terribly poor" because they had a love of home and were good companions.

5. Give reasons why you think the old man and the boy were "good citizens."

    The boy and the old man were good citizens because they had a love of home and were faithful to the simple duties.

6. Can we judge the character of people by their treatment of dumb and helpless animals?

    We can judge the character of people by the way they treat their animals. If a person is kind and gentle to an animal, he would probably be kind and gentle to other people.

7. Can you give any instances which show that dogs are grateful for kindness?

    Dogs show gratefulness by being loyal to their owners. They will protect and work for their owners.

Find in the glossary the meaning of: league, rheumatism, Flanders.

Find in the glossary the pronunciation of: Patrasche.

A Boy's Song, p. 51*

1. **Which stanza does the picture on page 51 (right) illustrate?**

   The picture illustrates the first stanza.

2. **Rhymes are organized in patterns called rhyme schemes: lines that rhyme are assigned the same letters of the alphabet beginning with the letter A. The first stanza has been done for you. Do all the stanzas follow the same rhyme scheme?**

Where the pools are bright and deep	**A**
Where the gray trout lies asleep	**A**
Up the river and o'er the lea,	**B**
That's the way for Billy and me.	**B**

   Yes, all the stanzas in the poem follow the same rhyme scheme.

3. **What do Billy and the speaker like to trace?**

   They like to trace the homeward bee.

Find in the glossary the meaning of: lea, nestlings, clustering.

Extended activity:

Have students write a poem about their favorite activities and places. For a challenge have students write their poem with four stanzas following an AABB rhyme scheme.

*This selection does not have "Helps to Study" questions in the reader.

A BOY'S SONG, P. 51

1. Which stanza does the picture on page 51 illustrate?

_____

2. Rhymes are organized in patterns called rhyme schemes: lines that rhyme are assigned the same letters of the alphabet beginning with the letter A. The first stanza has been done for you. Do all the stanzas follow the same rhyme scheme?

A Boy's Song

Where the pools are bright and deep,	**A**	Where the mowers mow the cleanest,	___
Where the gray trout lies asleep,	**A**	Where the hay lies thick and greenest,	___
Up the river and o'er the lea,	**B**	There to trace the homeward bee,	___
That's the way for Billy and me.	**B**	That's the way for Billy and me.	___
Where the blackbird sings the latest,	___	Where the hazel bank is steepest,	___
Where the hawthorn blooms the sweetest,	___	Where the shadow falls the deepest,	___
Where the nestlings chirp and flee,	___	Where the clustering nuts fall free,	___
That's the way for Billy and me.	___	That's the way for Billy and me.	___

—*James Hogg*

3. What do Billy and the speaker like to trace?

_____

_____

Extended activity:

On a separate sheet of paper, write a poem about your favorite activities and places. For a challenge write your poem with four stanzas following an AABB rhyme scheme.

No Boy Knows, p. 52

1. **What does the first stanza tell you that boys may know?**

    The first stanza tells us that boys may know "Who made the world in the dark and lit the great sun up."

2. **What things are mentioned in the second stanza that boys may know?**

    The second stanza tells us that boys "may know that the round old earth rolls east," and the stanza tells us about the earth's water cycle.

3. **"Ever repeating their parts again"—the poet thinks of the world as a play on a stage: the raindrops, the snowflakes, the ice—all are thought of as actors in a play, with their parts to act over and over again.**

4. **What do the sunbeams do with the water which they "sip" from the earth?**

    The sunbeams "sip" the water from the earth then pour the water back to earth.

5. **"Till the low streams leap"—till the shallow streams become filled with rain water, and rush along.**
    "Long, glad while"—a long, happy time.

6. **"Since the dawn's first smile"—since he was born, or first saw the light.**

7. **The poet speaks of the "dawn" as if it were a person smiling. Do you like this fancy?**

    Answers will vary.

8. **Do you think the woods are so beautiful that the poet may speak of them as a "divine," or heavenly, place?**

    Answers will vary.

9. **"Followed me o'er and o'er"—called up past memories again and again throughout his life.**

10. **Has your mother ever "pleaded" with you when you did not want to hear her?**

    Answers will vary.

A FAREWELL, P. 53*

1. **Why do you suppose "no lark could pipe to skies so dull and gray"?**

   The daughter's departure makes the parent sad. The parent's mood is compared to dull and gray skies. It is easier to sing a happy song when the skies are clear and blue.

2. **Put in your own words the advice the poet gives: "Do noble things, not dream them."**

   Answers will vary. One must act upon his dreams if they are to come true.

3. **As learned in "A Boy's Song," rhymes are organized in patterns called rhyme schemes: lines that rhyme are assigned the same letters of the alphabet beginning with A. What is the rhyme scheme of this poem?**

   My fairest child, I have no song to give you;   A
   No lark could pipe to skies so dull and gray;   B
   Yet, ere we part, one lesson I can leave you   A
   For every day.   B
   The second stanza follows the same rhyme scheme—ABAB

Find in the glossary the meaning of: pipe, clever, vast.

This selection does not have "Helps to Study" questions in the reader.

A FAREWELL, P. 53

1. Why do you suppose "no lark could pipe to skies so dull and gray"?

_____

_____

2. Put in your own words the advice the poet gives: "Do noble things, not dream them."

_____

_____

_____

3. Rhymes are organized in patterns called rhyme schemes: lines that rhyme are assigned the same letters of the alphabet beginning with A. What is the rhyme scheme of this poem?

A Farewell

My fairest child, I have no song to give you;   ____
No lark could pipe to skies so dull and gray;   ____
Yet, ere we part, one lesson I can leave you   ____
For every day.   ____

Be good, sweet maid, and let who will be clever;   ____
Do noble things, not dream them, all day long;   ____
And so make life, death, and that vast forever   ____
One grand, sweet song.   ____

—*Charles Kingsley*

WHAT THE WOOD-FIRE SAID, p. 54*

1. **To whom is the wood in the fire speaking?**
   It is speaking to the "little boy of the golden hair."

2. **For whom does the wood provide shelter?**
   It provides shelter for the "sweet bird."

3. **Who dreamed at the wood's feet?**
   The "beautiful meadows" dreamed at the wood's feet.

4. **What did the wood do to help the wandering birds?**
   It gave them shelter from the storm by rocking them to sleep.

5. **What eventually happened to the wood?**
   It got chopped down with an ax.

6. **At the end of the poem the wood turns its negative circumstance into something positive. Find the lines that show this change of attitude in the wood.**
   "Yet still there must be Some sweet mission for me, For have I not warmed you and cheered you tonight?"

7. **Personification is when human qualities are given to non-human objects. For example in the line "The wood said, 'See what they've done to me!'" The wood, a non-human object, is speaking or doing something only a human can do. Name two other examples of personification in the poem.**
   Possible answers: "The winds that went over the clover and wheat told me all that they knew," and "In the beautiful meadows that dreamed at my feet."

Find in the glossary the meaning of: myriad, shorn, mission.

This selection does not have "Helps to Study" questions in the reader.

WHAT THE WOOD-FIRE SAID, p. 54

1. To whom is the wood in the fire speaking?

_____

2. For whom does the wood provide shelter?

_____

3. Who dreamed at the wood's feet?

_____

4. What did the wood do to help the wandering birds?

_____

5. What eventually happened to the wood?

_____

6. At the end of the poem the wood turns its negative circumstance into something positive. Find the lines that show this change of attitude in the wood.

_____

_____

7. Personification is when human qualities are given to non-human objects. For example in the line "The wood said, 'See what they've done to me!'" the wood, a non-human object, is speaking or doing something only a human can do. Name two other examples of personification in the poem.

_____

_____

PIONEER TALES, p. 57

1. **Why did Crockett go on the dangerous trip to his brother-in-law's?**

    Crockett went on the dangerous trip to his brother-in-law's house because he was out of gun powder which he needed to hunt. The family was also getting low on meat.

2. **Read aloud lines which show that Crockett was thoughtful of his family; that he did not fear danger and pain; that he was determined to overcome difficulties:**

    "I knew the stream, which I would have to cross, as at least a mile wide, as the water was from hill to hill, and yet I was determined to go on over in some way or other so as to get my powder. I told this to my wife, but she opposed it with all her might. I still insisted…"

3. **Read lines that tell how Crockett kept himself from freezing.**

    "I now thought I would run, so as to warm myself a little…"

    "I knew I should freeze if I didn't warm myself in some way by exercise. So I would jump up and down with all my might, and throw myself into all sorts of motions."

4. **Compare Lincoln's and Roosevelt's handicaps with those of Crockett.**

    Roosevelt's handicap was different from Crockett's. Crockett seems to have had a strong body and Roosevelt had a weak body. Crockett is more like Lincoln who had a strong body.

5. **Read the last paragraph of the Forward Look, page 15, and tell us what we owe to pioneers like Crockett.**

    We owe "peace and comfort" to the "brave men and women who long ago toiled to make this country a safe, prosperous home…"

Find in the glossary the meaning of: thicket, slough, pursued.

EARLY SETTLERS, p. 63

1. **How long did this journey take?**

   The journey of the settlers took from May to the first of September.

2. **What things that now make travel easy were unknown then?**

   Things like cars and airplanes that make travel easy were unknown then.

3. **Find a sentence in the fourth paragraph of the story that shows how thrifty the early settlers were obliged to be. Are Americans as thrifty today?**

   A sentence in the fourth paragraph that shows how thrifty the settlers were is "A basket which has been accidentally dropped must be gone after, for nothing that they have can be spared."

   Answers will vary. Americans today are not as thrifty as the settlers were. Often times it is more convenient and cheaper to buy a new product rather than to save it and fix it.

4. **These were settlers in the warm southwest; do you think they had more or fewer hardships than settlers in the northwest?**

   The settlers in the warm southwest probably had an easier life than those in the northwest. The southwestern people did not have to deal with the snow and ice for as long, and they had more opportunity to plant gardens and crops.

Find in the glossary the meaning of: provisions, loom, canebrake, ammunition, ague, hoarfrost, felled, freshet, embark.

Extended Activities:

1. Have students complete the following activity. Pretend you are going on a car trip across the country from Pennsylvania to

California. Using a map chart your course. What states will you cross through and on what highways? What kinds of things will you pack? Make a list of those items. Pretend it will take you seven days to travel that distance. Write a daily journal of the things you see along the way and include illustrations/photos. Students can use the log on page 38 for their journal entries.

2. Have students look at a map of the United States and make a list of states that would be considered the "warm southwest" and those that would be considered the "cold northwest." Then have students mark on the map where they live. Write a paragraph explaining the weather pattern where they live.

EARLY SETTLERS, p. 63

1. Complete the following activity. Pretend you are going on a car trip across the country from Pennsylvania to California. Using a map chart your course. What states will you cross through and on what highways? What kinds of things will you pack? Make a list of those items. Pretend it will take you seven days to travel that distance. Write a daily journal of the things you see along the way and include illustrations/photos.

2. Look at a map of the United States and make a list of states that would be considered the "warm southwest" and those that would be considered the "cold northwest." Mark on the map where you live. Write a paragraph explaining the weather pattern where you live.

TRAVELOG

Day _____

Traveled from _____

To _____

What I saw:

DANIEL BOONE, p. 66

1. **"Account for each ball"—the Indians made Boone show some piece of game killed by each ball they had given him. What does this prove about his wonderful ability to shoot accurately?**

   The fact that every ball could be matched with an animal shows Daniel Boone was an excellent marksman, always hitting his target.

2. **How did he manage to save some ammunition for his own use?**

   Boone was able to save some ammunition for his own use by using half a ball to kill turkeys, raccoons, and other small game.

3. **What did he do when he found that the Indians were making "preparations for the warpath," that is, getting ready to attack the white men?**

   When Boone found out the Indians were getting ready to attack the white men, he escaped while hunting and traveled 160 miles to warn the fort at Boonesborough.

4. **After reading this selection can you give some reasons why Boone is remembered and admired?**

   Boone is remembered and admired because of his bravery and dedication to helping fellow pioneers.

5. **What do we owe to men like Boone?**

   We owe our peace and comfort to men like Daniel Boone.

Find in the glossary the meaning of: garrison, outwitted, vigorous, athletic.

THE FIRST THANKSGIVING,

p. 70

1. **On page 77, what did the father say should make the Plymouth settlers happy?**

   On page 77, Father says finding freedom should make the Plymouth settlers happy.

2. **For what other blessing were they thankful?**

   The settlers were thankful for the Indians' help in teaching them to catch eel and lobster. They were also thankful to the Indians for teaching them how to grow and cook maize.

3. **What have you to be grateful for on Thanksgiving day?**

   Answers will vary.

4. **On page 16 you read that "work and thrift" make happy, useful citizens. Find several speeches in this story which prove that Plymouth colonists believed in the truth of this statement.**

   Several speeches that prove the colonists believed "work and thrift" make happy, useful citizens are:

   page 71, Mother: "The best cure for sorrow is work."

   page 78, Mother: "He who eats must first earn."

5. **Choose characters, and dramatize the story for a Thanksgiving play.**

Find in the glossary the meaning of: samp, grief, matchlock, maize, journey-cake, trenchers, pewter.

PROVERBS OF SOLOMON, P. 83*

1. **Solomon was the third and last king of united Israel. He was the author of three books of the Bible: Song of Solomon, Proverbs and Ecclesiastes. Solomon is most noted for his wisdom.**

2. **For each stanza, write Solomon's words of wisdom in your own words.**

   Answers will vary, but the content should reflect the following:

   He that gathereth in summer is a wise son;
   But he that sleepeth in harvest is a son that causeth shame.
   - It is wise to work and shameful to be lazy.

   A good name is rather to be chosen than great riches,
   And loving favor rather than silver or gold.
   - One's reputation is more valuable than material wealth.

   A righteous man regardeth the life of his beast;
   But the tender mercies of the wicked are cruel.
   - One can judge a man's character by the way he treats his animals.

   A faithful witness will not lie;
   But a false witness will utter lies.
   - One cannot trust people who lie.

   A soft answer turneth away wrath,
   But grievous words stir up anger.
   - One will get ahead in life by speaking kind words. Hurtful words cause conflicts.

   A wise son maketh a glad father;
   But a foolish man despiseth his mother.
   - A father finds comfort in a wise son and only a fool does not appreciate his mother.

   Pride goeth before destruction,
   And a haughty spirit before a fall.
   - Pride and arrogance can often lead to one's downfall.

3. **Choose a proverb and write a story in which the characters learn the value of the proverb.**

Find in the glossary the meaning of: mercies, utter, haughty.

This selection does not have "Helps to Study" questions in the reader.

PROVERBS OF SOLOMON, P. 83

For each stanza, write Solomon's words of wisdom in your own words.

He that gathereth in summer is a wise son;
But he that sleepeth in harvest is a son that causeth shame.

_____

_____

A good name is rather to be chosen than great riches,
And loving favor rather than silver or gold.

_____

_____

A righteous man regardeth the life of his beast;
But the tender mercies of the wicked are cruel.

_____

_____

A faithful witness will not lie; But a false witness will utter lies.

_____

_____

A soft answer turneth away wrath, But grievous words stir up anger.

_____

_____

A wise son maketh a glad father; But a foolish man despiseth his mother.

_____

_____

Pride goeth before destruction, And a haughty spirit before a fall.

_____

_____

Choose a proverb and write a story in which the characters learn the value of the proverb.

Story	Find in the glossary the meaning of:
Reader p. 17	**quarters**_____
	rebels_____
Reader p. 21	**corporal**_____
	fortified_____
	breastwork_____
Reader p. 23	**guidon**_____
Reader p. 24	**franc**_____
	consul_____
	Lafayette_____
	respect_____
	justice_____
Reader p. 27	**dispute**_____
Reader p. 29	**perseverance**_____
	poverty_____
Reader p. 32	**stalwart**_____
	Cher Ami_____
Reader p. 37	**content**_____
Reader p. 38	**elderbloom**_____
	delicate_____
	toil_____
	humble_____
Reader p. 40	**mink**_____
	lowing_____
	milch_____
	heifer_____
	tranquil_____
	drowsily_____
	repose_____
	co', boss_____
Reader p. 42	**league**_____
	rheumatism_____
	Flanders_____
Reader p. 51	**lea**_____
	nestlings_____
	clustering_____
Reader p. 53	**pipe**_____
	clever_____
	vast_____

Pronounce:
Cornwallis, revolution, Patrasche

PART II:
FAIRYLAND AND ADVENTURE

In This Section—

These stories and poems do not have "Helps to Study" questions in the reader. However, questions have been added in this teacher's guide to address those selections. These additional questions appear on separate worksheets which may be copied for the students.

**The first number refers to the page in the reader on which the story begins; the second refers to the page in the "Helps to Study" section in the back of the student's reader where the pertinent questions appear.*

Objectives—

By completing "Part II," the following objectives will be met.

1. The student will use effective reading strategies to construct meaning and identify purpose of text including:
    a. using illustrations
    b. defining unfamiliar words
    c. retelling and summarizing
2. The student will determine the main idea or essential message and identify relevant supporting details and facts of a text.
3. The student will read and organize facts from the text and other sources to make a report, and outline and perform an authentic task.
4. The student will prepare for writing by focusing on the topic and organizing supporting details in a logical sequence.
5. The student will draft and revise writing in cursive.
6. The student will produce final documents that have been edited for correct spelling and punctuation.
7. The student will write for a variety of audiences and purposes.
8. The student will write in a variety of genres including narration, exposition, and poetry.
9. The student will use speaking strategies effectively such as using eye contact and gestures that engage the audience.
10. The student will be familiar with the common features of fiction and nonfiction.
11. The students will understand morals that help to develop good character through the reading of fables.

THROUGH THE LOOKING-GLASS, p. 87

1. **Alice has been playing chess, a game played with pieces called kings, queens, etc., then she sits by the fire before the looking-glass. She imagines that there is a house behind the glass and wishes she could visit it. Then she falls asleep and dreams that she goes through the looking-glass, into the Looking-Glass World. In this world she finds living chess queens. After many adventures she becomes a queen.**

2. **Alice expects things to happen as they do in her own world, but nothing happens as she expects. This makes the fun of the book; read aloud the lines that gave you the heartiest laugh.**

   Answers will vary but may include some of the following:
   - "But if everybody obeyed that rule, and if you only spoke when you were spoken to, and the other person always waited for you to begin, you see nobody would ever say anything, so that—"
   - "What's one and one and one and one and one and one and one and one and one and one?"
   - "The bone wouldn't remain, of course, if I took it—and the dog wouldn't remain; it would come to bite me—and I'm sure I shouldn't remain!"

Find in the glossary the meaning of: timidly, interrupted, argument, ridiculous, conversation, pleaded, piteous, complain of, vicious, opportunity, cautiously, triumphantly, emphasis, circumstances, anxiously, consequences, venture, clever, perplexity.

Extended Activities:

1. Alice says, "It's exactly like a riddle with no answer!" Have students list some of the riddles the queens ask her. Ask students to write an answer to the questions. Answers will vary:
   - "What do you suppose is the use of a child without any meaning?"
   - "Can you do subtraction? Take nine from eight."

- "Divide a loaf by a knife—what's the answer to that?"
- "Take a dog from a bone; what remains?"
- "How is bread made? Where do you pick the flower? How many acres are ground?"
- "What's the French for fiddle-de-dee?"
- "What is the cause of lightning?"

2. Have students name some events that happen differently than Alice expects. Possible answers:

Alice never expects to be a queen so soon, and to have a party and not invite her own guests. She also never expects that queens have days and nights in sets of two, three, or five, and that she'd have to take care of two queens asleep at once.

THROUGH THE LOOKING-GLASS, p. 87

1. Alice says, "It's exactly like a riddle with no answer!" List some of the riddles the queens ask her. Write an answer to the questions.

   "What do you suppose is the use of a child without any meaning?"

   _____

   _____

   "Can you do subtraction? Take nine from eight."

   _____

   _____

   "Divide a loaf by a knife—what's the answer to that?"

   _____

   _____

   "Take a dog from a bone; what remains?"

   _____

   _____

   "How is bread made? Where do you pick the flower? How many acres are ground?"

   _____

   _____

   "What's the French for fiddle-de-dee?"

   _____

   _____

   "What is the cause of lightning?"

   _____

   _____

2. Name some events that happen differently than Alice expects.

   _____

   _____

   _____

THE QUANGLE WANGLE'S HAT, p. 96

1. **The author of this nonsense verse "makes" some new words for our amusement, such as "bibbons"; find others.**
   Other new words for our amusement include:
   Crumpetty Tree, Quangle Wangle Quee, Fimble Fowl, Pobble, Dong, Land of Tute, Attery Squash, Bisky Bat.

2. **Which fancy of the poet gave you the heartiest laugh?**
   Students will have various answers that may include:
   • "For his Hat was a hundred and two feet wide,
   With ribbons and bibbons on every side
   And bells, and buttons, and loops, and lace
   So that nobody ever could see the face
       Of the Quangle Wangle Quee."

   • "When all these creatures move
   What a wonderful noise there'll be!"

3. **Find the lines that rhyme. [Rhymes are organized in patterns called rhyme schemes: lines that rhyme are assigned the same letters of the alphabet beginning with A. (For an example refer to Part I "A Farewell" question #3, page 35, *Teacher's Guide*.)]**
   The rhyme scheme is as follows: Stanza 1 - ababccdda; stanza 2 - eaeaaaffa; stanza 3 - aaaabbgga; stanza 4 - ahahiibba; stanza 5 - jkjkllbba; stanza 6 - eamannaaa

4. **Read the poem aloud, to bring out its musical quality.**

Find in the glossary the meaning of: luminous.

Extended Activities:

Dr. Seuss was well-known for his poems with made-up words. Assign one of his poems and have the students find the created words and rhyme scheme.

THE QUANGLE WANGLE'S HAT, p. 96

Dr. Seuss was well-known for his poems with made-up words. Take one of his poems and find the created words and rhyme scheme.

Poem: _____

Rhyme Scheme: _____

Created Words:

_____

_____

_____

_____

_____

_____

_____

_____

_____

_____

_____

_____

RUMPELSTILTSKIN, P. 99*

1. **What kind of character was the miller?**

   The miller was boastful. He pretended to be someone important when he met the king, bragging that his daughter could spin straw to gold. He regretted his boasting when the king demanded to see his daughter.

2. **Find and read some statements that describe Rumpelstiltskin's character.**
   - "Tell me what is the matter, and I will try to help you."
   - "He had a kind heart, and he thought he would give the queen one more chance."
   - "He had brought a soft white blanket to wrap the baby in, for he was kindhearted and did not want it to catch cold."

3. **The miller's daughter was taken to a room full of straw and told to spin it to gold. Think of a time when you or someone you know faced a task that seemed impossible. How was the task completed? Write in cursive an explanation of your answer.**

4. **If a magician showed up in your room and could perform any task, what task would you want him to perform? Write in cursive an explanation of your answer.**

Find in the glossary the meaning of: clever, glistening, curious, anxious.

Find in the glossary the pronunciation of: Rumpelstiltskin.

Extended Activity:

   Have students read through books of magic tricks and learn how to perform one. Have students demonstrate their skills to the class.

This selection does not have "Helps to Study" questions in the reader.

RUMPELSTILTSKIN, P. 99

1. What kind of character was the miller?

_____

_____

_____

2. Find and read some statements that describe Rumpelstiltskin's character.

_____

_____

_____

3. The miller's daughter was taken to a room full of straw and told to spin it to gold. Think of a time when you or someone you know faced a task that seemed impossible. How was the task completed? Write in cursive an explanation of your answer.

_____

_____

_____

4. If a magician showed up in your room and could perform any task, what task would you want him to perform? Write in cursive an explanation of your answer.

_____

_____

_____

_____

Read through books of magic tricks and learn how to perform one. Demonstrate your skill to the class.

THE WISE JACKAL, p. 107*

1. **To what things did the brahman speak on his way to the village?**

    The brahman spoke to a fig tree, a buffalo, a road, and a jackal.

2. **Which one saved his life and how did he do it?**

    The jackal saved his life by pretending to be ignorant and tricked the tiger into entering the cage. The jackal fastened the door and caught the tiger.

3. **An important rule for getting along with others is to treat them as you want to be treated. Did the fig tree, the buffalo, and the road follow that advice?**

    No, they all complained that men mistreated them, but they also mistreated the brahman.

4. **Have you ever felt mistreated? How did you react? What kind of reaction shows good character?**

Find in the glossary the meaning of: repay, unjust, yoke, tread.

Find in the glossary the pronunciation of: brahman.

This selection does not have "Helps to Study" questions in the reader.

THE WISE JACKAL, p. 107

1. To what things did the brahman speak on his way to the village?

_____

_____

_____

2. Which one saved his life and how did he do it?

_____

_____

_____

3. An important rule for getting along with others is to treat them as you want to be treated. Did the fig tree, the buffalo, and the road follow that advice?

_____

_____

_____

4. Have you ever felt mistreated? How did you react? What kind of reaction shows good character?

_____

_____

_____

_____

_____

_____

_____

_____

THE FOOLISH JACKAL, p. 112*

1. **Why was the jackal in this story called foolish?**
    He was foolish because he did not treat the camel with respect, even though the camel was his friend.

2. **Read the story "The Wise Jackal" and explain how these two jackals were different.**
    The wise jackal helped someone in need even though he was a stranger. The foolish jackal did not help his own friend.

3. **"The Foolish Jackal" is an old Indian tale known as a fable, a folk story told over and over to entertain and teach the reader a moral or lesson about life. Read these morals and explain what lessons we could learn from the "The Foolish Jackal."**
    A. Actions speak louder than words.
    Moral—just saying you are friends isn't enough; you have to show it by your actions. The jackal didn't do that.
    B. Get a taste of your own medicine.
    Moral—you get back what you give. The jackal got the camel in trouble, so the camel dumped him in the water to show him what it felt like to be betrayed by a friend.
    C. Do unto others as you would have them do to you.
    Moral—treat others with respect. The jackal did not respect the camel.
    D. Don't bite the hand that feeds you.
    Moral—appreciate what others do for you. The camel carried the jackal safely across the water, but the jackal was ungrateful for his help.

Find in the glossary the meaning of: arouse.

This selection does not have "Helps to Study" questions in the reader.

THE FOOLISH JACKAL, p. 112

1. Why was the jackal in this story called foolish?

    _____

    _____

    _____

2. Read the story "The Wise Jackal" and explain how these two jackals were different.

    _____

    _____

    _____

3. "The Foolish Jackal" is an old Indian tale known as a fable, a folk story told over and over to entertain and teach the reader a moral or lesson about life. Read these morals and explain what lessons we could learn from the "The Foolish Jackal."

    A. Actions speak louder than words.

    _____

    _____

    B. Get a taste of your own medicine.

    _____

    _____

    C. Do unto others as you would have them do to you.

    _____

    _____

    D. Don't bite the hand that feeds you.

    _____

    _____

THE PORCELAIN STOVE, p 114

1. **Notice that this story has five parts: with the help of four classmates, tell the story, each one telling one of the parts.**

   The five parts of the story to be presented include: August's Home, The Stove is Sold, August Goes With the Stove, The Stove is Sold Again, August Before the King.

2. **In what ways is this a different kind of story from "Rumpelstiltskin"?**

   This is a different kind of story from Rumplestiltskin in the following ways: In "Rumpelstiltskin," the miller had a lovely girl, a magician saved the girl, and Rumpelstiltskin did not get his reward. In "The Porcelain Stove," the father had a lovely stove, August saved the stove, and August got his reward—the stove.

3. **Do you think August was foolish to take the dangerous trip inside the stove, or do you admire him for his faithfulness to the thing he loved?**

   Answers will vary.

Find in the glossary the meaning of: twilight, porcelain, hues, potter, sledges, breathless, enamel, flaw, husky, florin, jesting, heaved, museum, hobbled, shrewd, fretwork, tortures, bric-a-brac, ledge, exclamations, ducats, rogues, ill-gotten.

In the glossary find the pronunciation of: Hirschvogel, Augustin.

Extended Activities:

Like a web, a Venn Diagram is a graphic organizer. Venn Diagrams help students to organize information and to visualize similarities and differences between two items or concepts. Unique characteristics of the items or concepts being analyzed are listed in the outer circles and common features are listed in the overlapping part of the circles. Have students draw a Venn Diagram to compare and contrast "The Porcelain Stove" to "Rumplestiltskin."

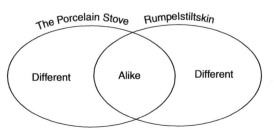

THE PORCELAIN STOVE, P. 114

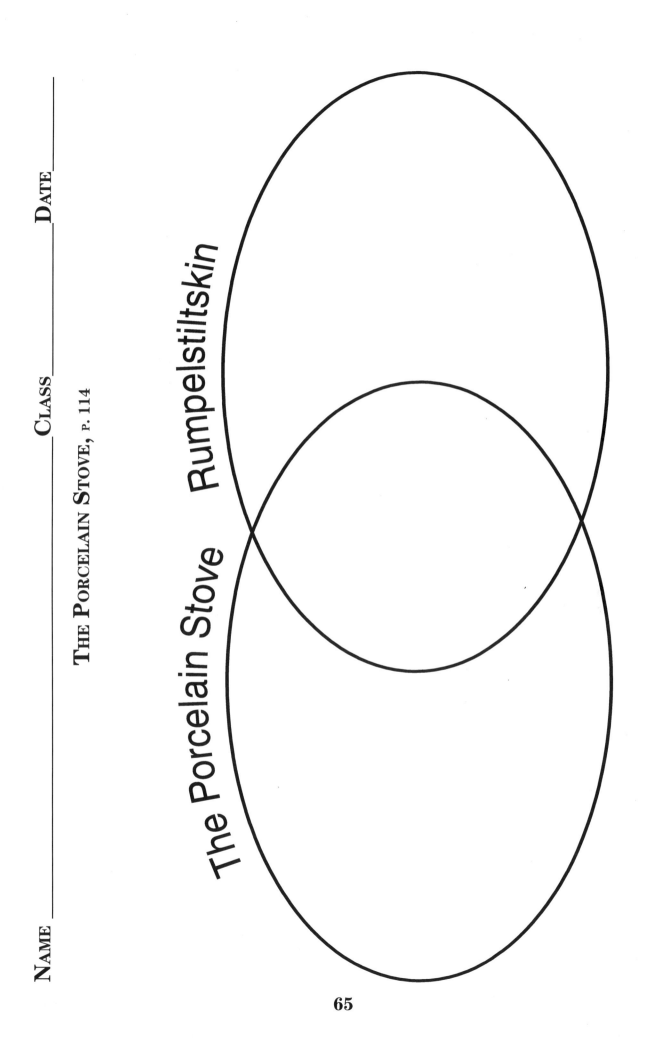

The Porcelain Stove

Rumpelstiltskin

THAT CALF, p. 134*

1. **Read the sentence that explains the old farmer's problem in this story.**

   "Now which of you, last night, shut the barn door while I was in bed?"

2. **Whom did all the animals blame?**

   All the animals blamed the calf.

3. **In the discussion section of "The Foolish Jackal," you read about the moral of a story—a message meant to teach the reader a lesson. How does the moral, "Honesty is the best policy" fit this story?**

   The calf answered honestly that she had shut the door. The farmer rewarded her with praise.

4. **Read the lines that show how the calf's honesty paid in the end.**

   "Come here, little bossy, my dear! You have done what I cannot repay, and your fortune is made from today."

5. **How did the animals behave after the farmer praised the calf?**

   The animals all pretended to be her friend.

6. **Another famous old saying is "Eat humble pie." How did the animals prove this moral?**

   They had to "eat" their words, which accused the calf of shutting the door.

7. **How did the calf respond to the animals' sudden praise?**

   "But that calf only answered them, "Boo!"

In the glossary find the meaning of: recollect, suspect, brindle, repay, foundered.

This selection does not have "Helps to Study" questions in the reader.

THAT CALF, p. 134

1. Read the sentence that explains the old farmer's problem in this story.

_____

_____

2. Whom did all the animals blame?

_____

_____

3. In the discussion section of "The Foolish Jackal," you read about the moral of a story—a message meant to teach the reader a lesson. How does the moral, "Honesty is the best policy" fit this story?

_____

_____

_____

4. Read the lines that show how the calf's honesty paid in the end.

_____

_____

_____

5. How did the animals behave after the farmer praised the calf?

_____

_____

6. Another famous saying is "Eat humble pie." How did the animals prove this moral?

_____

_____

7. How did the calf respond to the animals' sudden praise?

_____

_____

AGREED TO DISAGREE, p. 136*

1. **Read the lines that
    tell why the mouse did not like the cricket's house.**
    "Oh, dear, I fear, I fear such a place would be so dark and
    drear!"

2. **Read the lines that tell why the cricket did not like the
    bumblebee's house.**
    "Why, as I cannot fly, I never could think of going so high."

3. **Read the lines that tell why the bumblebee did not like
    the mouse's house.**
    "Dear me, dear me! Such a house would never do for three."

4. **In the story of "The Foolish Jackal" and "That Calf"
    you learned several phrases or morals that teach the
    reader a lesson. Read these phrases and explain what
    they teach us in the poem "Agreed to Disagree."**

    A. A place for everything and everything in its place.
    Moral—each of us has a place that's right for us; we should not
    expect others to do things our way. The mouse, the cricket
    and the bumble bee all agreed to stay in their own place.
    B. There's no place like home.
    Moral—others might have some things you want, but your
    own life is still the best for you. The animals decided to stay
    in their own homes built for their needs.
    C. All's well that ends well.
    Moral—if you agree to disagree, everyone can end up being
    happy. "And though they could never live together, All
    rejoiced in the sweet spring weather."

This selection does not have "Helps to Study" questions in the reader.

AGREED TO DISAGREE, p. 136

1. Read the lines that tell why the mouse did not like the cricket's house.

   _____

   _____

2. Read the lines that tell why the cricket did not like the bumblebee's house.

   _____

   _____

3. Read the lines that tell why the bumblebee did not like the mouse's house.

   _____

   _____

4. In the story of "The Foolish Jackal" and "That Calf" you learned several phrases or morals that teach the reader a lesson. Read these phrases and explain what they teach us in the poem "Agreed to Disagree."

   A. A place for everything and everything in its place.

   _____

   _____

   B. There's no place like home.

   _____

   _____

   C. All's well that ends well.

   _____

   _____

A BRAVE BOY'S ADVENTURE, p. 138

1. **This selection is from a story of the Revolutionary War. Robinson was on the American side; on which side were the Ramsays?**

   The Ramsays were on the American side.

2. **What soldiers wore "red coats" in this war?**

   The British soldiers wore red coats.

3. **Read aloud lines that show how Robinson tried to make the soldiers believe he had a large force with him.**

   "Keep them outside the door—stand fast!" "Sir," he said turning to the young officer, "you must see that it is not worth fighting five to one. I should be very sorry to be the death of any of your brave fellows; so, take my advice, and surrender to this scrap of the American army which I command."

4. **What did Andy do that helped Robinson in this plan?**

   "Come on, boys!" he shouted, as he turned his face toward the field. "Shall I let loose upon them, Captain?" While Horseshoe was speaking, the lad outside was calling out, first on one name, and then on another, as if in the presence of a troop."

5. **"Rights of prisoners of war"—in all wars, prisoners have the right to be treated with respect.**

6. **How did the soldiers feel when they saw the "troop" that had captured them?**

   Their first feelings were of great anger, which were followed by laughter from one or two of them. Then they looked at each other, slyly, in a way that showed a purpose to turn upon their captors.

7. **Why did Robinson make the British soldiers lead the way?**

   Robinson made the British soldiers lead the way so they would not turn on him. He could keep his eyes on them at all times.

8. Choose characters and dramatize the story, using the dialogue form in the text as far as possible.

Find in the glossary the meaning of: artillery, corps, ensign, swaggering, rioters, heeding, sturdy, scrimmage, desperate, threshold, mounted, steed, superior, post, captors, resist, submitted, preserved, venturesome.

Find in the glossary the pronunciation of: revolutionary.

THE CHRISTMAS FAIRY AND SCROOGE, p. 148

1. Why did Scrooge call Christmas a "humbug"?

Scrooge called Christmas a "humbug" because he thought all enthusiasm and merrymaking was foolish—a waste of money and time.

2. Read what Scrooge's nephew said Christmas had done for him.

"Christmas is a kind time, a forgiving time. It is a time to think of those who need help. It is a time when people smile and say cheery words. I believe that Christmas has done me good and will do me good, and I say, 'God bless it!'"

3. What did Bob Cratchit have that Scrooge did not have?

The Fairy told Scrooge that Bob Cratchit had something better than sixpences; he had a kind and loving heart.

4. What did the fairy bring Scrooge for a Christmas gift?

The Fairy told Scrooge, "You need a kind and loving heart. I will help you get it."

5. What does Act I tell you? Act II? Act III?

Act I: Scrooge is introduced as a mean, miserly gentleman with no desire to celebrate Christmas. He refuses his nephew's invitation to Christmas dinner and scolds him for suggesting that Scrooge help Cratchit's family. The Christmas Fairy appears and repeats the nephew's request to help Cratchit. Again Scrooge refuses and demands that the Fairy leave. She refuses to go saying she has brought him a gift.

Act II: The Fairy magically transforms Scrooge's living room into Cratchit's home, where his family is enthusiastically preparing Christmas dinner. Scrooge watches as they discuss his stingy, selfish behavior.

Act III: The scene returns to Scrooge's living room where the Fairy and Scrooge discuss the Cratchit family. Scrooge recognizes his meanness and promises to raise Cratchit's wages and help Tiny Tim. He has learned the lesson of Christmas—love and kindness are more valuable than money.

6. **What change came over Scrooge?**

   A change came over Scrooge when he asked the Fairy to change his hard heart for a kind one.

7. **What caused this change?**

   The change in Scrooge was caused by seeing the Cratchit family. Their happiness in spite of their poverty softened his cold, mean heart.

8. **Choose characters and dramatize this story for a Christmas play.**

Find in the glossary the meaning of: scowling, humbug, sixpence.

Extended Activities:

1. Have the students create art work/dioramas that depict some aspect of the story.

2. Have students write an essay persuading someone that giving is better than receiving. Have them plan their writing, write a draft, and proofread it for errors. Then have students write a final draft in cursive.

THE CHRISTMAS FAIRY AND SCROOGE, p. 148

1. Create artwork or a diorama that depicts some aspect of the story.

2. Write and essay persuading someone that giving is better than receiving. Plan your writing. Write a draft (below) and proofread it for errors. Then write a final draft in cursive.

_____

_____

_____

_____

_____

_____

_____

_____

_____

_____

_____

_____

_____

_____

_____

_____

_____

_____

_____

_____

Story	Find in the glossary the meaning of:
Reader p. 87	**timidly**_____
	interrupted_____
	argument_____
	ridiculous_____
	conversation_____
	pleaded_____
	piteous_____
	complain of_____
	vicious_____
	opportunity_____
	cautiously_____
	triumphantly_____
	emphasis_____
	circumstances_____
	anxiously_____
	consequences_____
	venture_____
	clever_____
	perplexity_____
Reader p. 96	**luminous**_____
Reader p. 99	**clever**_____
	glistening_____
	curious_____
	anxious_____
Reader p. 107	**repay**_____
	unjust_____
	yoke_____
	tread_____
Reader p. 112	**arouse**_____
Reader p. 114	**twilight**_____
	porcelain_____
	hues_____
	potter_____
	sledges_____
	breathless_____
	enamel_____
	flaw_____
	husky_____
	florin_____

jesting_____

heaved_____

museum_____

hobbled_____

shrewd_____

fretwork_____

tortures_____

bric-a-brac_____

ledge_____

exclamations_____

ducats_____

rogues_____

ill-gotten_____

Reader p. 134 recollect_____

suspect_____

brindle_____

repay_____

foundered_____

Reader p. 138 artillery_____

corps_____

ensign_____

swaggering_____

rioters_____

heeding_____

sturdy_____

scrimmage_____

desperate_____

threshold_____

mounted_____

steed_____

superior_____

post_____

captors_____

resist_____

submitted_____

preserved_____

venturesome_____

Reader p. 148 scowling_____

humbug_____

sixpence_____

Pronounce:

Rumpelstiltskin, brahman, Hirschvogel, Augustin, revolutionary.

PART III:
THE WORLD OF NATURE

In This Section—

These stories and poems do not have "Helps to Study" questions in the reader. However, questions have been added in this teacher's guide to address those selections. These additional questions appear on separate worksheets which may be copied for the students.

**The first number refers to the page in the reader on which the story begins; the second refers to the page in the "Helps to Study" section in the back of the student's reader where the pertinent questions appear.*

Objectives—

By completing "Part III," the following objectives will be met.

1. The student will use a glossary to determine meaning and increase vocabulary.
2. The student will clarify comprehension by summarizing and checking other sources.
3. The student will read text to determine main ideas, identify supporting details, and arrange events in chronological order.
4. The student will read and organize information for a variety of purposes including making a report.
5. The student will use the writing process effectively.
      (a) produce a document edited for conventions and format
      (b) organize information using alphabetical systems
6. The student will use speaking strategies effectively by using eye contact and gestures that engage the audience.
7. The student will understand the nature and power of language.
8. The student will request information from a civic group using appropriate level of formality.
9. The student will understand the common features of a variety of literary forms.
10. The student will identify and use literary terminology including alliteration, consonance, onomatopoeia, and personification.
11. The student will recognize cause-and-effect relationships in literary texts.

PLANTING THE TREE, p. 165

1. **What are some of the things that are made from the wood of a tree?**

   From the wood of a tree we build: ships with masts, planks, keel, keelson, beam, knee; houses with rafters, shingles, floors, studding, laths, doors, beams, siding; in addition, we build spires, staffs, and shade.

2. **"All parts that be"—all the different parts there are.**

3. **What day is set apart for one of our duties toward trees?**

   Arbor Day was established in 1872 to remind us to plant and care for trees. Each region of the United States observes Arbor Day at a different time depending on their region's most appropriate planting season.

4. **How can we help to protect our trees?**

   We can help protect trees by: providing good soil and sufficient water sources; trimming trees to develop full leafy branches; protecting them from insects and diseases; controlling air pollution that threatens their health.

5. **In the "Forward Look," page 164, you read, "Mother Nature is the most wonderful of magicians." How does the poem you have just read prove the truth of this statement?**

   Mother Nature provides the raw materials that help us survive. From housing to food, from jobs to recreation we find Mother Nature at work "magically" providing our needs.

Find in the glossary the meaning of: gales, keelson, knee, rafters, studding, laths, beam, spire, out-towers, crag.

Extended Activities:

1. Have students research Arbor Day to discover its goals.

2. Have students write a business letter to ask for information regarding Arbor Day. One organization to contact would be the National Arbor Day Foundation, 100 Arbor Ave., Nebraska City, NE 68410. Have students research the Internet for other possible organizations.

3. Have students plant a tree in honor of Arbor Day.

PLANTING THE TREE, p. 165

1. Research Arbor Day to discover its goals.

   _____

   _____

   _____

   _____

2. Write a business letter to ask for information regarding Arbor Day. One organization to contact would be the National Arbor Day Foundation, 100 Arbor Ave., Nebraska City, NE 68410. Research the Internet for other possible organizations.

How the Leaves Came Down, p. 166*

1. **What names did the Tree call his children?**
   The Tree called them Yellow, Brown, and Red.

2. **Read the lines that suggest the leaves were like real children at bedtime.**
   The leaves were like real children when they begged to stay and play.
   "Ah! begged each silly, pouting leaf.
   Let us a little longer stay;
   Dear Father Tree, behold our grief!
   'Tis such a pleasant day
   We do not want to go away."

3. **How did the Tree finally send them to bed?**
   The Tree "shook his head, and far and wide, Fluttering and rustling everywhere, Down sped the leaflets through the air."

4. **Who was the "one from far away" who came to "wrap them safe and warm"?**
   The one from far away was the snow with "white bedclothes heaped upon her arm."

5. **Summarize "How the Leaves Came Down" by creating a comic strip that illustrates the main idea of the poem beginning with the leaves on the tree and ending with the leaves in bed.**

Find in the glossary the meaning of: huddled, swarm.

*This selection does not have "Helps to Study" questions in the reader.

HOW THE LEAVES CAME DOWN, p. 166

1. What names did the Tree call his children?

   _____

2. Read the lines that suggest the leaves were like real children at bedtime.

   _____

   _____

   _____

   _____

   _____

3. How did the Tree finally send them to bed?

   _____

   _____

   _____

4. Who was the "one from far away" who came to "wrap them safe and warm"?

   _____

   _____

   _____

5. Summarize "How the Leaves Came Down" by creating a comic strip that illustrates the main idea of the poem beginning with the leaves on the tree and ending with the leaves in bed.

MAY, p. 168*

1. **In "Part I" in the discussion of "What the Wood-Fire Said," (page 37 in *Teacher's Guide*), you read that personification is a figure of speech that gives human qualities to non-human objects. When we say, "The leaves skipped across the grass," we see the leaves performing the human action of skipping, and we are using personification. List some examples of personification in this poem.**

Non-human object	*Human action*
May	skipped into the woods
She (May)	teased the brook
Brook	laughed and gurgled and scolded
She (May)	chirped to the birds
Birds	sang a chorus of welcome
Bees and butterflies	woke the sleeping flowers
She (May)	shook the trees
Buds	looked to see what the trouble was all about

2. **Why is May said to have a life-giving touch?**
    May has a life-giving touch because she wakes up the creatures that have slept through the winter, getting them to laugh, sing, and grow again.

3. **Draw a picture of bees and butterflies waking sleeping flowers.**

*This selection does not have "Helps to Study" questions in the reader.

MAY, p. 168

1. **Personification is a figure of speech that gives human qualities to non-human objects. When we say, "The leaves skipped across the grass," we see the leaves performing the human action of skipping, and we are using personification. List some examples of personification in this poem.**

Non-human object   *Human action*

_____   _____

_____   _____

_____   _____

_____   _____

_____   _____

_____   _____

_____   _____

2. **Why is May said to have a life-giving touch?**

_____

_____

_____

_____

3. **Draw a picture of bees and butterflies waking sleeping flowers.**

TALKING IN THEIR SLEEP, P. 168*

1. **Whom did the apple tree pity?**
    The apple tree pitied the grass.
    Whom did the grass pity?
    The grass pitied the flower.
    How did the flower respond to their pity?
    The flower told them,
    "You will see me again—I shall laugh at you then,
    Out of the eyes of a hundred flowers."

2. **How does the title "Talking in Their Sleep" fit this poem?**
    "Talking in Their Sleep" is a good title because the apple tree, the grass, and the flowers all appeared to be dead, but they were really just asleep, waiting for spring so they could sprout again. They were only talking in their sleep.

3. **Using crayons, color the part of the Venn Diagram with colors we see in the fall; with colors we see in the spring. Do the two seasons have any colors in common?**

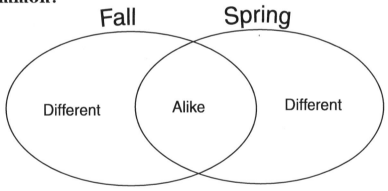

Find in the glossary the meaning of: plumy.

Extended Activity:

The flower says, "I never have died, But close I hide In the plumy seed...." Have the student plant a flower seed and see if the flower was right when it said, "You will see me again."

This selection does not have "Helps to Study" questions in the reader.

TALKING IN THEIR SLEEP, p. 168

1. **Whom did the apple tree pity?**

   _____

   Whom did the grass pity?

   _____

   How did the flower respond to their pity?

   _____

   _____

   _____

   _____

   _____

2. **How does the title "Talking in Their Sleep" fit this poem?**

   _____

   _____

   _____

   _____

3. **Using crayons, color the part of the Venn Diagram with colors we see in the fall; with colors we see in the spring. Do the two seasons have any colors in common?**

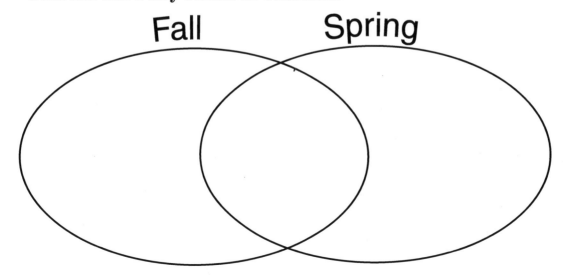

Fall   Spring

THE TREE, p. 170*

1. **Stanzas are lines of poetry grouped together that express a single idea. Each stanza is separated from other stanzas by a space. What season of the year is reflected in the first stanza when the frost spoke to the tree?**

    Spring is reflected in the first stanza when the "early leaf buds were bursting their brown."

2. **What season of the year is reflected in the second stanza when the wind spoke to the tree?**

    Early summer is reflected in the second stanza when the "tree bore his blossoms."

3. **Finally, what season of the year is reflected in the last stanza when the girl spoke to the tree?**

    The girl spoke to the tree in the "midsummer glow" when the berries were ripe.

Find in the glossary the meaning of: crown, quivering, laden.

*This selection does not have "Helps to Study" questions in the reader.

THE TREE, p. 170

1. Stanzas are lines of poetry grouped together that express a single idea. Each stanza is separated from other stanzas by a space. What season of the year is reflected in the first stanza when the frost spoke to the tree?

   _____

   _____

2. What season of the year is reflected in the second stanza when the wind spoke to the tree?

   _____

   _____

3. Finally, what season of the year is reflected in the last stanza when the girl spoke to the tree?

   _____

   _____

THE SQUIRRELS AT WALDEN, p. 171

1. **The picture (right) shows the cabin that Thoreau built in the woods, where he lived two years, studying the animals and the birds and the trees.**

2. **How did Thoreau "bait" the squirrels?**

   Thoreau baited the squirrels by throwing out ears of corn on the snow for them.

3. **Why does he speak of the squirrel as an "impudent" fellow?**

   The squirrel is impudent because he climbs to the top of the woodpile outside Thoreau's window, looks him in the face, and nibbles at the ears of corn, throwing around the half-eaten ears.

4. **Tell what you have learned about squirrels from this selection.**

   Answers will vary but may include the concepts that squirrels are fast, frisky, and friendly. References in the story to support those answers are: his wonderful speed, his behavior on the woodpile, and his fearlessness of humans when he stepped on the poet's shoes on his way to gather food.

Find in the glossary the meaning of: baited, warily, wager, zigzag, strewn, familiar.

How the Chipmunk Got Its Stripes, p. 173*

1. **Describe the geloori's appearance at the beginning of the tale before he met Shiva.**
   The geloori was a little gray chipmunk with a bushy tail.

2. **What was the geloori doing when he met Shiva?**
   The geloori was dipping his tail into the sea and shaking out the water on the shore.

3. **What was the geloori trying to accomplish?**
   The geloori was trying to drain the sea so his wife and children could escape from their nest in the palm tree that had blown into the sea.

4. **How did the geloori's appearance change after he met Shiva?**
   After Shiva stroked his fur, the geloori found four green stripes on his fur, the marks of Shiva's fingers.

5. **The marks on the gelorri's fur were signs of love. How did Shiva show his love for the geloori?**
   He showed his love by rescuing the geloori's family from drowning.

6. **How did the geloori show his love for his family?**
   He showed his love by trying to save his family, even though he faced the impossible task of draining the sea alone.

7. **Can you think of a time when someone who loved you helped you solve a problem you faced?**

Find in the glossary the pronunciation of: geloori, Shiva.

This selection does not have "Helps to Study" questions in the reader. These additional questions may be copied for the student from sheet provided.

HOW THE CHIPMUNK GOT ITS STRIPES, p. 173

1. Describe the geloori's appearance at the beginning of the tale before he met Shiva.

_____

2. What was the geloori doing when he met Shiva?

_____

_____

3. What was the geloori trying to accomplish?

_____

_____

4. How did the geloori's appearance change after he met Shiva?

_____

_____

5. The marks on the geloori's fur were signs of love. How did Shiva show his love for the geloori?

_____

_____

6. How did the geloori show his love for his family?

_____

_____

7. Can you think of a time when someone who loved you helped you solve a problem you faced?

_____

_____

THE BLUEBIRD, p. 175*

1. **What message did the bluebird bring?**

   The bluebird sang a message of cheer, "Summer is coming! and springtime is here!"

2. **How many different spring flowers can you identify in this poem?**

   Four spring flowers are listed: the snow-drop, crocus, violets, and daffodils.

3. **In Part I of this reader you read the poem on page 53 called "A Farewell." You were encouraged to find the lines that rhymed by labeling each line with a letter; lines that rhymed received the same letter. What is the rhyme scheme or pattern for "The Bluebird"?**

   The rhyme scheme for this poem is as follows: stanza 1 - aabb; stanza 2 - ccdd; stanza 3 - eeff; stanza 4 - gghhff.

   How does the last stanza's rhyme scheme differ from the first three stanzas?

   The last stanza has two additional lines that rhyme.

This selection does not have "Helps to Study" questions in the reader.

THE BLUEBIRD, p. 175

1. What message did the bluebird bring?

_____

_____

2. How many different spring flowers can you identify in this poem?

_____

3. In Part I of this reader you read the poem on page 53 called "A Farewell." You were encouraged to find the lines that rhyme by labeling each line with a letter; lines that rhymed received the same letter. What is the rhyme scheme or pattern for "The Bluebird"?

Stanza 1_____

Stanza 2_____

Stanza 3_____

Stanza 4_____

How does the last stanza's rhyme scheme differ from the first three stanzas?

_____

_____

_____

THE SINGING LESSON, p. 176*

1. **In stanza one, what mistake did the nightingale make?**
   She sang notes out of tune.

2. **What actions did she take that showed her shame?**
   She hid from the moon, wrung her claws, tucked her head under her wing, and pretended to sleep.

3. **In stanza two, the dove compares the nightingale to three other types of birds. Which birds and why?**
   The dove compared her to: a goose because she was being silly; a common fowl (like a chicken) who scatters and runs when it is frightened; an owl who buries his head under his wing.

4. **In stanza three, what advice did the dove have for the nightingale?**
   The dove told her to be proud of herself and think of what she could do if she tried.

5. **Stanza five ends with these lines: "And this story's a moral, I know, If you'll try to find it out." What is the moral of this story?**
   The moral reminds us to use the gifts we have to do our best, no matter how afraid we might be or how we think people may respond.

Find in the glossary the meaning of: skulk, contemptible, crest, divine, ascended, moral.

This selection does not have "Helps to Study" questions in the reader.

THE SINGING LESSON, p. 176

1. In stanza one, what mistake did the nightingale make?

_____

_____

2. What actions did she take that showed her shame?

_____

_____

3. In stanza two, the dove compares the nightingale to three other types of birds. Which birds and why?

_____

_____

4. In stanza three, what advice did the dove have for the nightingale?

_____

_____

5. Stanza five ends with these lines: "And this story's a moral, I know, If you'll try to find it out." What is the moral of this story?

_____

_____

_____

_____

Humility, p. 177*

1. **Find in the glossary the definition of humility.**

   The definition of humility is meekness.

2. **After reading the poem, can you explain why the poet says, "What honor hath humility"?**

   Answers will vary, but the poet says that the soaring bird, such as the lark, nests on the ground and the singing bird, such as the nightingale, performs in the shade (night) when other creatures rest. This suggests that honor comes from doing our job well, even though it may not be glamorous or noticed by others.

This selection does not have "Helps to Study" questions in the reader.

HUMILITY, P. 177

1. Find in the glossary the definition of humility.

_____

_____

2. After reading the poem, can you explain why the poet says, "What honor hath humility"?

_____

_____

_____

_____

_____

_____

_____

_____

_____

_____

_____

BOB WHITE, p. 178

1. **Why does the poet say "stacked is the corn" when he means "the corn is stacked"?**
    The poet arranges the words so that corn and morn rhyme.
    Find another sentence in this poem that shows the same unusual order of words.
    Another sentence with unusual word order is, "Ah! I see why he calls; in the stubble there Hide his plump little wife and babies fair!"

2. **At what season and time does Bob White whistle?**
    Bob White whistles on fall mornings when the buckwheat is ripe, the corn is stacked, and there are billows of gold and amber grain.

3. **What does he whistle?**
    He whistles, "Bob White! Bob White! Bob White!"

4. **Read aloud the words that tell why he calls.**
    "So contented is he! and so proud of the same, That he wants all the world to know his name."

5. **Why do you think he is a vain little bird?**
    He's vain because he chirps his own name repeatedly.

Find in the glossary the meaning of: remote, bracy, blithe, billows, stubble.

BEES AND FLOWERS, p. 179

1. **In the "Forward Look," page 164, you were told that to learn the secrets of nature you would need to listen to the words of the "wise storytellers of nature," keeping "your eyes wide open and your ears alert." What "secrets" did you learn from "The Bees and the Flowers"?**

   Answers may vary but should include the idea that bees keep to one kind of flower on each trip from the hive. Flowers depend on bees to carry their pollen to and from other plants. Flower colors and scents are nature's traps to attract insects.

2. **What does the bee do for the plant in return for the honey?**

   The bee carries pollen for the flowers which makes stronger and better flowers.

3. **Why do some flowers have bright colors?**

   The bright colors attract insects who carry the pollen dust to other flowers.

4. **What experiment did Sir John Lubbock make? (It is doubtful whether this single experiment really proves that bees can tell one color from another.)**

   He placed honey on pieces of glass and laid them on colored paper. After the bees identified the honey with the color, he switched the honey to another color. When the bees returned to the same color to find their honey, it was gone, so they followed the scent to a new color.

5. **Why do some flowers close when the rain comes?**

   Some flowers close so the rain will not spoil their honey.

Find in the glossary the meaning of: leisurely, mignonette, pollen dust, ornamental.

THE BEE AND THE FLOWER, p. 182*

1. **Onomatopoeia is the use of a word that sounds like its meaning, as in swish, boom, bang. Find two examples of onomatopoeia in the poem.**

    Two examples of onomatopoeia are "buzzed" and "hum."

2. **We use consonance when we repeat consonant sounds in words that are close together. Find examples of consonance in the poem.**

    Words showing consonance include come, come, hum; flower was withered.

3. **Write a poem using at least one example of onomatopoeia and one example of consonance.**

*This selection does not have "Helps to Study" questions in the reader.

THE BEE AND THE FLOWER, p. 182

1. Onomatopoeia is the use of a word that sounds like its meaning, as in swish, boom, bang. Find two examples of onomatopoeia in the poem.

_____

_____

2. We use consonance when we repeat consonant sounds in words that are close together. Find examples of consonance in the poem.

_____

_____

_____

3. Write a poem using at least one example of onomatopoeia and one example of consonance.

_____

_____

_____

_____

_____

_____

_____

_____

_____

_____

_____

_____

TAKING LUNCH WITH A WILD GROUSE, p. 183

1. **This is a true story written by the well-known lover of birds who organized the Bird Club of Long Island, New York, May 14, 1915. Colonel Theodore Roosevelt was made president of this club.**

2. **Tell of the author's first visit to the grouse.**

   On the author's first visit, the grouse walked down the hill to meet him. When she reached her guest, she stopped and looked at him, but when he tried to touch her she drew back her head, raised her neck feathers and pecked his hand. Later she hopped onto his shoulder and ate wild raspberries from his fingers.

   Of his visit on the following day.

   The next day when the author arrived, he brought a basket of raspberries and thumped his chest as he approached her. She soon came running to him and they sat under an oak tree where the grouse ate raspberries from the author's knees. When the author tried to leave, the grouse jumped on his feet and pecked his trousers. When the author began to run, the grouse flew into his ribs to stop him and march him back to their starting place. Later the author and his guests spread a blanket under the trees and the grouse sat among them eating ripe raspberries from the bowl. When it was time to go, the grouse followed them for about 50 yards then stopped and watched them go on alone. The last her guests saw her she was walking slowly, head down, back to her woodland.

3. **What does the picture on page 186 (above) show you?**

   The picture describes the second visit when the guests spread the blanket on the ground and the grouse sat in the center eating berries from a bowl.

4. **This story shows that birds will be our friends if we encourage them; what can we do to make them our friends?**

   We can treat them with kindness by not startling or shooing them away. We can encourage their trust with bits of their favorite foods.

5. **What can we do to protect the birds?**

   Their natural habitats are being destroyed by the spread of cities and highways. We can build refuges for them, a refuge as simple as a birdhouse in our back yards. We can enforce laws that protect various species of birds; we can provide food and shelter by planting trees and shrubs that produce berries and provide nesting areas. Since flowers attract insects that birds like to eat, we can plant flowers. In addition, we can provide water for drinking and bathing.

6. **Do you feed the birds in winter?**

   Answers will vary.

Find in the glossary the meaning of: ruffed grouse, partridge, persisted, wistful.

Find in the glossary the pronunciation of: Oneonta.

THE CHILD'S WORLD, p. 187*

1. **In the first stanza, the poet describes the world using a variety of adjectives. List the adjectives he uses.**
    The adjectives are: great, wide, beautiful, wonderful.
    What are the world's clothes?
    The world's clothes are the wonderful water and the wonderful grass.

2. **In stanza two, the poet uses personification to describe the wind. (Refer to "What the Wood-Fire Said," *Teacher's Guide,* page 37, for a definition of personification.) What actions does the wind perform?**
    The wind shakes the tree, walks on water, whirls the mills, and talks to itself.

3. **In stanza three, the poet identifies various nouns— people, places, things, and ideas—that you can find on the earth. What are they?**
    The poet mentions wheat fields, cities, gardens, cliffs, isles, and people.

4. **Finally in stanza four, the author identifies the greatest thing in the world. What is it and why?**
    The greatest thing in the world is a child because a child can love and think, and the earth cannot.

Find in the glossary the meaning of: cliffs, isles.

This selection does not have "Helps to Study" questions in the reader.

THE CHILD'S WORLD, p. 187

1. In the first stanza, the poet describes the world using a variety of adjectives. List the adjectives he uses.

_____

_____

_____

   What are the world's clothes?

_____

_____

2. In stanza two, the poet uses personification to describe the wind. What actions does the wind perform?

_____

_____

3. In stanza three, the poet identifies various nouns—people, places, things, and ideas—that you can find on the earth. What are they?

_____

_____

4. Finally in stanza four, the author identifies the greatest thing in the world. What is it and why?

_____

_____

THE BROOK-SONG, p. 188

1. **How did the poet learn so much about the brook?**
    When the poet was a boy, he often skipped school to come and
        listen to the brook.

2. **What songs does the poet ask the brook to sing?**
    He asks the brook to sing about a bumblebee, a leaf, a dragonfly,
        and happiness.

3. **"One and one"—one by one, coming quickly after each
        other.**

4. **What does he say the "ripples" are like?**
    Ripples are like laughing children in the rain.

5. **What do you think it was that made the "dreamer"
        sad?**
    Answers will vary but may include the idea that the dreamer
        is now a grown person who perhaps regrets some wrong
        choices or perhaps has lost a dream or person close to him.

6. **Who do you think the "dreamer" was?**
    Perhaps the dreamer was once the little boy in the poem, now
        a grown man who dreams of his childhood.

7. **Read aloud the lines in which he tells the brook how to
        keep the "dreamer" from weeping.**
    "Sing him all the songs of summer till he sink in softest sleep;
        And then sing soft and low
        Through his dreams of long ago—
            Sing back to him the rest he used to know!"

**Find in the glossary the meaning of: swerve, crook, ripples,
    film, current, glee, lilting, refrain, wrought.**

THE RIVULET, p. 189*

1. **Your glossary describes a rivulet as a stream or brook. Where does the rivulet run?**

   The rivulet runs through the meadow, the forest (pines), the waterfall, the fields of flowers, the city, the mountains, hills, and finally to the sea.

2. **Which lines rhyme?**

   In each stanza, lines one, two, and five rhyme, and lines three and four rhyme.

3. **Create a piece of art that shows the travels of the rivulet.**

Find in the glossary the meaning of: delicate.

This selection does not have "Helps to Study" questions in the reader.

THE RIVULET, p. 189

1. Your glossary describes a rivulet as a stream or brook. Where does the rivulet run?

_____

_____

_____

2. Which lines rhyme?

_____

_____

3. Create a piece of art that shows the travels of the rivulet.

RAINING, p. 190*

1. **The poet says the rain is raining flowers. How many different flowers does he identify?**
    The poet sees daffodils, wild flowers, roses, clover, and violets.

2. **Where can the bees find a place to rest?**
    The bees find a bed in the fields of clover.

3. **How does the poet describe the bee?**
    The poet says the bee is buccaneering—or robbing—the flowers.

4. **Read the poem "The Bee and the Flower" on page 182 to see what the bee is robbing.**
    The bee is robbing honey from the flowers.

5. **In the discussion questions of "The Bee and the Flower" you learned that consonance refers to repeated consonant sounds in words. Another term for repeated consonant sounds is alliteration—consonants repeated at the beginnings of words such as "Peter Piper picked a peck of pickled peppers." How many examples of alliteration can you find in the poem "Raining"?**
    Alliterations include: raining rain (four times), dimpled drop, raining roses, buccaneering bee, health happy, fig frets.

*This selection does not have "Helps to Study" questions in the reader.

RAINING, p. 190

1. The poet says the rain is raining flowers. How many different flowers does he identify?

_____

_____

2. Where can the bees find a place to rest?

_____

3. How does the poet describe the bee?

_____

4. Read the poem "The Bee and the Flower" on page 182 to see what the bee is robbing.

_____

5. In the discussion questions of "The Bee and the Flower" you learned that consonance refers to repeated consonant sounds in words. Another term for repeated consonant sounds is alliteration— consonants repeated at the beginnings of words such as "Peter Piper picked a peck of pickled peppers." How many examples of alliteration can you find in the poem "Raining"?

_____

_____

_____

_____

_____

_____

_____

A WONDERFUL WEAVER, p. 191*

1. **What is the weaver?**
   The weaver is the snow.
   What does he weave?
   He weaves a white mantle for the earth, bush, and tree; a cover for the meadow; a cap for the pillar and post; and changes the pump to a ghost.

2. **What does the sun do to the weaver's work?**
   The sun unravels it all, or melts it.

3. **Look up the word "loom" in an encyclopedia. Sketch a picture of a loom.**

Find in the glossary the meaning of: mantles, shuttle, loom, decks, flinty, quaint, grim.

*This selection does not have "Helps to Study" questions in the reader.

A WONDERFUL WEAVER, p. 191

1. What is the weaver?

_____

What does he weave?

_____

_____

2. What does the sun do to the weaver's work?

_____

_____

3. Look up the word "loom" in an encyclopedia. Sketch a picture of a loom.

MISHOOK, THE SIBERIAN CUB, p. 192*

1. **The setting of a story is the time and place in which the action of the story occurs. Where and at what time of year is the setting for this story?**

   The setting is a den in the Siberian Forest. It is March, still cold and snowy when the story begins.

   Find Siberia on a map.

2. **Describe Mishook and his little sister.**

   They were both tiny and covered with thick, dark brown fur except for a ring of white fur around their necks. They had narrow blunt noses, small round ears, short tails, and sharp claws on their toes.

3. **What does the picture on page 196 (above) show you?**

   On Mishook's first walk, he became very frightened when he saw his brother and sister climbing high up in a tree.

4. **What clues did the hunters look for when tracking the bears?**

   They looked for the stain of the bears' warm breath on the white snow.

5. **A few times in this story, events occur that cause Mother Bruin to slap her cubs' ears. What were the events and what did the cubs learn?**

   The older cub lost his patience while watching Mishook and slapped him so hard that Mishook cried. Mother Bruin "flew at her elder son and boxed his ears soundly." Another time the elder cub wandered away looking for berries, leaving Mishook and his sister alone. Once again Mother Bruin slapped her elder cub.

6. **A time line helps the reader keep track of the main events in a story. Complete the following time line to show the most important events in each of the chapters in Mishook's life.**

   Time Line:
   A. In the Den_____

   B. The First Walk_____

   C. Getting Ready For Winter_____

   D. The Bear Hunt_____

   E. Mishook's New Home_____

   F. In the Forest Again_____

Answers will vary but should reflect the following ideas.

A. In the Den—Mishook, his twin sister, and his older brother and sister lived with their mother in a den, sleeping through the cold winter.

B. The First Walk—Mishook and his sister learned to climb trees and hunt for food. He got his first taste of honey and bee stings.

C. Getting Ready For Winter—Mother Bruin killed a horse, and later other village animals, so her babies would have meat to fatten their skinny bodies for the long cold winter ahead.

D. The Bear Hunt—The hunters tracked down Mother Bruin and killed her.

E. Mishook's New Home—Mishook and his family were separated, and he went to live with his new owner, an army officer. One day he bit a soldier's hand.

F. In the Forest Again—Mishook was taken back to the forest where he came from, and he was once again free and wild.

7. **Design questions from your time line that you can use to quiz your classmates.**

Find in the glossary the meaning of: muzzles, ravine, Siberian, zoological gardens, captivity.

This selection does not have "Helps to Study" questions in the reader.

MISHOOK, THE SIBERAN CUB, p. 192

1. The setting of a story is the time and place in which the action of the story occurs. Where and at what time of year is the setting for this story?

_____

_____

Find Siberia on a map.

2. Describe Mishook and his little sister.

_____

_____

_____

3. What does the picture on page 196 show you?

_____

_____

4. What clues did the hunters look for when tracking the bears?

_____

5. A few times in this story, events occur that cause Mother Bruin to slap her cubs' ears. What were the events and what did the cubs learn?

_____

_____

_____

_____

6. A time line helps the reader keep track of the main events in a story. Complete the following timeline to show the most important events in each of the chapters in Mishook's life.

Timeline:

A. In the Den_____

_____

B. The First Walk_____

_____

C. Getting Ready For Winter_____

_____

D. The Bear Hunt_____

_____

E. Mishook's New Home_____

_____

F. In the Forest Again_____

_____

7.   Design questions from your time line that you can use to quiz your classmates.

_____

_____

_____

_____

_____

_____

_____

_____

THE MONTHS: A PAGEANT, P. 204*

1. **Notice that each month brings some message of good cheer or kindness. Which month do you think brings the happiest message?**
    Answers will vary.

2. **March says, "The violet is born where I set the sole of my flying feet." Does the violet come as March leaves, in your region?**
    Answers will vary.

3. **"Has not a fellow," page 211—has no equal.**

4. **"Hard upon," page 211—close behind.**

5. **"Recovered calm," page 211—the quiet that has returned after the storm.**

6. **"Men are brethren of each other," etc., page 212—men belong to the same family of human beings, and are almost brothers of the animals ("litter") and birds ("brood") that have to struggle against ("breast" here means to meet bravely) the cold wind and disagreeable weather just as human beings do.**

7. **"Pearled with dew," page 213—the drops of dew on the skin of the palm look like pearls.**

8. **What does November mean by saying that the earth will "wake to mirth by and by"?**
    Winter will pass and spring will come again, bringing happiness to the world.

9. **"My short days end," etc., page 216—When in December is the shortest day of the year?**
    The shortest day of the year is December 21 or 22, the first day of winter when the sun reaches the solstice, its most southern position.

10. Memorize December's cheery speech.

Find in the glossary the meaning of: pageant, fagot, embers, plodding, waistcoat, loitering, rend, catkins, bower, bliss, waxing, linnets, hedges, lulled, scatheless, balm, canary, savory, litter, brood, sear, lamenting, pall, grim, dismal, nought, hoar frost, aglow.

Extended Activities:

1. In discussion question one, students read that each month brings some message of good cheer or kindness. Have the students identify the cheer or kindness in each month.

a) January brings Robin Redbreast a breakfast of crumbs.
b) February brings a snowdrop to prove the world is awake.
c) March winds bring flowers and music from the forests.
d) April brings hope and sweetness.
e) May brings more flowers and singing birds.
f) June brings strawberries.
g) July brings peaches.
h) August brings grain for bread.
i) September brings plums, pears, apples, melons, figs, and damsons.
j) October brings nuts.
k) November brings pine cones for warmth.
l) December brings a holly wreath and lengthening days.

2. With their classmates have students act out "The Months" following the drama directions as described in the poem.

3. Have students choose their favorite season, then contrast it with the opposite season. A Venn Diagram could be used.

4. Have students draw a picture of the month of their birthday.

THE MONTHS: A PAGEANT, P. 204

1. Notice that each month brings some message of good cheer or kindness. Which month do you think brings the happiest message?

_____

_____

2. March says, "The violet is born where I set the sole of my flying feet." Does the violet come as March leaves, in your region?

_____

8. What does November mean by saying that the earth will "wake to mirth by and by"?

_____

_____

9. "My short days end," etc., p. 216—When in December is the shortest day of the year?

_____

_____

10. Memorize December's cheery speech.

Extended Activites:

1. In discussion question one, you read that each month brings some message of good cheer or kindness. Identify the cheer or kindness in each month.
   January_____
   February_____
   March_____
   April_____
   May_____
   June_____
   July_____
   August_____
   September_____
   October_____

November_____

December_____

3. **Choose your favorite season, then contrast it with the opposite season. Use the Venn diagram below.**

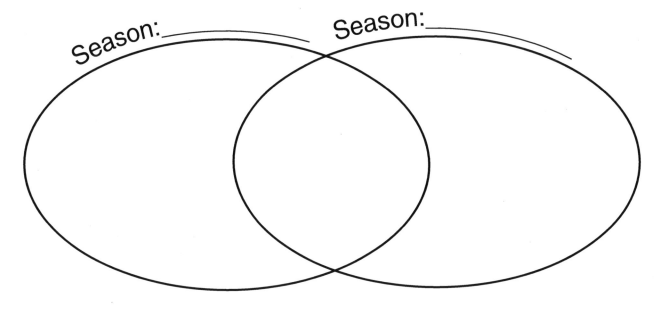

4. **Draw a pciture of the month of your birthday.**

Story	Find in the glossary the meaning of:
Reader p. 165	**gales**_____
	keelson_____
	knee_____
	rafters_____
	studding_____
	laths_____
	beam_____
	spire_____
	out-towers_____
	crag_____
Reader p. 166	**huddled**_____
	swarm_____
Reader p. 168	**plumy**_____
Reader p. 170	**crown**_____
	quivering_____
	laden_____
Reader p. 171	**baited**_____
	warily_____
	wager_____
	zigzag_____
	strewn_____
	familiar_____
Reader p. 173	**geloori**_____
	Shiva_____
Reader p. 176	**skulk**_____
	contemptible_____
	crest_____
	divine_____
	ascended_____
	moral_____
Reader p. 178	**remote**_____
	bracy_____
	blithe_____
	billows_____
	stubble_____
Reader p. 179	**leisurely**_____
	mignonette_____
	pollen dust_____
	ornamental_____

balm_____

canary_____

savory_____

litter_____

brood_____

sear_____

lamenting_____

pall_____

grim_____

dismal_____

naught_____

aglow_____

Pronounce:
geloori, Shiva, Oneonta.

Part IV:
Famous Heroes of Long Ago

In This Section—

** *The first number refers to the page in the reader on which the story begins; the second refers to the page in the "Helps to Study" section in the back of the student's reader in which the pertinent questions appear.*

† *See "Suggestions for Silent Reading" on page 3.*

125

Objectives—

By completing "Part IV," the following objectives will be met.

1. The student will use effective reading strategies to construct meaning and identify purpose of text including:
    - a. using illustrations
    - b. defining unfamiliar words
    - c. retelling and summarizing
2. The student will determine the main idea or essential message and identify relevant supporting details and facts of a text.
3. The student will read and organize facts from the text and other sources to make a report and outline and perform an authentic task.
4. The student will prepare for writing by focusing on the topic and organizing supporting details in a logical sequence.
5. The student will draft and revise writing in cursive.
6. The student will produce final documents that have been edited for correct spelling and punctuation.
7. The student will write for a variety of audiences and purposes.
8. The student will write in a variety of genres including narration, exposition, and poetry.
9. The student will use speaking strategies effectively such as using eye contact and gestures that engage the audience.
10. The student will be familiar with the common features of fiction and nonfiction.
11. The student will identify the development of plot and how conflicts are resolved in a story.
12. The student will identify and understand similarities and differences among the characters, settings, and events presented in various texts.
13. The student will identify and use literary terminology such as rhyme scheme and personification.
14. The student will respond critically to fiction, nonfiction, poetry, and drama.
15. The student will recognize cause-and-effect relationships in literary texts.
16. The student will respond to a text by explaining how the motives of the characters or events compare with those in his or her own life.

BEOWULF, THE BRAVE PRINCE P. 221†

King Hrothgar's Hall

1. **How did King Hrothgar show his love for his warriors?**

   He built them a great hall where he fed his warriors and entertained them.

2. **Who was Grendel, and what did he do?**

   Grendel was a mean giant who was jealous of the king and his warriors. He came to the hall one night and killed thirteen men. Afterward the men quit coming to the hall at night, but Grendel would hide and terrorize the men. For twelve years the Danes suffered from Grendel.

The Coming of Beowulf

1. **When Beowulf heard the story of the wicked Grendel, what did he decide to do?**

   Beowulf decided to go to King Hrothgar and help him by slaying Grendel.

2. **How many warriors did he take with him?**

   Beowulf took fifteen warriors with him.

3. **How did King Hrothgar welcome Beowulf and his warriors?**

   King Hrothgar welcomed Beowulf and his warriors by providing them with a big feast.

Beowulf's Battle with Grendel

1. **Give an account of Beowulf's battle with Grendel.**

   Beowulf waited for Grendel at night and attacked him. Grendel, wounded, ran away and threw himself in the lake and died.

2. **What answer did Beowulf make when the king told him to ask for any reward that he might desire?**

   "Not for reward did I come to this land, but to save thee from this terrible monster. Now that Grendel is dead and will nevermore trouble thee, I shall joyfully return home."

3. **Tell of the banquet.**

The Danes and Goths sat down together at the table. The "hall echoed with laughter and song, and the good king rejoiced to see people so happy."

4. **What gifts did the king present to Beowulf?**

The king gave Beowulf a "banner, a helmet, and a sword with a hilt of gold." He also gave him eight beautiful horses with harnesses of gold and one had a silver saddle.

The Second Monster

1. **How did the second monster trouble the Danes?**

He came up out of the lake, entered the hall, and killed one of the greatest warriors.

2. **What promise did Beowulf make to the king?**

"To rid thee of this enemy also."

The Battle under the Water

1. **Tell of Beowulf's battle under the water.**

"Backward and forward they struggled, in and out of the cave." Beowulf was losing strength when he saw a great sword. He seized it and struck the monster dead.

2. **Why did not Beowulf take the monster's gold?**

"Not for gold did I go down into that dreadful lake, but to save the people of this land."

Beowulf's Return Home

1. **What promise did he give King Hrothgar before he left?**

"If ever again I can help thee, my lord, I will come to thee with joy."

2. **How was he made welcome in his own country?**

The king invited him to sit beside him.

3. **What did he do with the presents King Hrothgar had given him?**

He gave them to his king and kept none for himself.

The Fiery Dragon

1. **Why did the Goths praise Beowulf?**
    They praised him for his bravery and courage.

2. **What honor was given him by the Goths?**
    They made him king.

3. **Why did the dragon set fire to the houses?**
    The dragon set fire to the houses because he knew someone came into his den and stole a cup.

Beowulf's Last Battle

1. **Tell of Beowulf's fight with the dragon.**
    Beowulf fought bravely. Wiglaf came to Beowulf's aid when the dragon took Beowulf in his mouth. Wiglaf struck the dragon making Beowulf fall. Beowulf was then able to hit the dragon and kill him.

Make an outline for the story, using subtitles as topics. Then choose eight of your classmates and, thinking of them as "minstrels," listen while they tell the complete story, each telling about one of the topics. (Formal outlines use Roman numerals for main topics. If students are not comfortable using Roman numerals have them use Arabic numbers or letters of the alphabet.)

    I. King Grothgar's Hall
    II. The Coming of Beowulf
    III. Beowulf's Battle with Grendel
    IV. The Second Monster
    V. The Battle Underwater
    VI. Beowulf's Return Home
    VII. The Fiery Dragon
    VIII. Beowulf's Last Battle

Find in the glossary the meaning of: minstrel, victorious, warriors, sentinel, Goths, foe, grasp, hilt, comrade.

Find in the glossary the pronunciation of: Hrothgar, Grendel.

Sigurd, the Youthful Warrior, p. 239†

Sigurd's Childhood

1. Who was Sigurd's father?

Sigurd's father was a brave warrior.

2. With whom did Sigurd and his mother live after the father died?

Sigurd lived with King Alf.

3. Why did Sigurd ask for his father's sword?

He wanted to be a brave warrior like his father and use his sword.

4. What advice was given Sigurd by his mother?

She told him to "be brave and true. Think not of thyself but always of others."

Regin, the Smith

1. How did Regin plan to make use of Sigurd?

Regin wanted to train Sigurd so he would go and fetch the treasure for him.

2. What did the king allow Regin to teach Sigurd?

Regin was to teach Sigurd his wisdom.

3. What did King Alf say Regin must not teach Sigurd?

He was not to teach hatred and deceit.

Sigurd's Horse

1. Why did Sigurd want a horse?

He wanted a horse so he could ride into battle.

2. Tell how Sigurd chose a horse.

He chased a group of wild horses into the river. The horse that swam across and back was the one Sigurd chose because he was a strong horse.

3. What advice did the old man give the boy?

"...think not of thyself nor fear for thy life."

Regin's Story

1. What was the story that Regin told Sigurd?

Regin told Sigurd that his father had much gold of which none was given to Regin. When Regin's father died, his brother took the gold. Years later a dragon came and was guarding the gold. He would not let anyone get to it.

2. Why did Sigurd promise to kill the dragon?

Sigurd said he would help Regin.

3. What reason did Sigurd give for wanting to slay the dragon?

"...to rid the world of the terrible monster."

Sigurd's Sword

1. Where did Sigurd find a sword?

Sigurd's mother gave him his father's sword. He took it to Regin who welded it together to make a fine sword for Sigurd.

2. What did he tell King Alf?

He told King Alf that he was going to "destroy a cruel dragon and to gain the treasure which he guards."

Sigurd Kills the Dragon

1. Give an account of Sigurd's search for the dragon, and of his killing it.

Sigurd left early in the morning. He went over the plains and through mountains to a great high plain. Then he went on foot tracking the dragon's foot prints. Then, while on the edge of a cliff, the dragon came to fight Sigurd. Sigurd struck him with his sword and the dragon died.

Sigurd Saves the Princess

1. **What wonderful thing happened after Sigurd had killed the dragon?**

   Sigurd could understand the birds' language.

2. **How did Sigurd pass through the wall of fire?**

   Sigurd put on a helmet and armor then rode his steed bravely through the fire.

3. **How did he wake Brunhild?**

   He woke Brunhild by taking off her heavy helmet and armor.

Make an outline for the story, using the subtitles as topics. Then choose seven of your classmates and, thinking of them as minstrels, listen while they tell the complete story, each telling about one of the topics. (Formal outlines use Roman numerals for main topics. If students are not comfortable using Roman numerals have them use Arabic numbers or letters of the alphabet.)

    I. Sigurd's Childhood
   II. Regin, the Smith
  III. Sigurd's Horse
   IV. Regin's Story
    V. Sigurd's Sword
   VI. Sigurd Kills the Dragon
  VII. Sigurd Saves the Princess

Find in the glossary the meaning of: regain, smithy, Denmark, forge, weld, toil, anvil, weapons.

Find in the glossary the pronunciation of: Sigurd, Brunhild.

ROLAND, THE NOBLE KNIGHT, p. 257†

Roland's Boyhood

1. **Where did Roland live when he was a little boy?**

   Roland lived in a cave on a hillside in Sutri, Italy.

2. **Who was his playmate and best friend?**

   His playmate and best friend was Oliver, the governor's son.

3. **Where had his mother once lived?**

   His mother once lived with her brother, King Charlemagne, in his palace.

4. **Why could not Roland have clothes as good as Oliver's?**

   He could not have nice clothes because they were poor. Roland's father had died.

Charlemagne Finds Roland

1. **How did Charlemagne find Roland?**

   Charlemagne was traveling through Italy when he came to Sutri. He set up tables of food for the people under the trees. Twice Roland came boldly and took some food for his mother. On the second occasion, Charlemagne followed Roland home.

Roland's New Home

1. **Where was Roland's home after he left the hillside?**

   He went to live with Charlemagne in his palace.

2. **What great service did he do for the king in his first battle?**

   Roland saved his life.

3. **Show that Roland was not boastful.**

   He would say, "It's nothing," when people praised him. He also told of battles fought by other warriors and told how proud he was of his comrades.

Charlemagne and Roland in Spain

1. **Where did Roland again meet Oliver?**

   He met Oliver again when Oliver came to help Charlemagne fight against the Saracens.

2. **How long did the war with the Saracens continue?**

   The war lasted seven years.

3. **What plan did the Saracen king make to deceive Charlemagne?**

   He gave Charlemagne gifts and told Charlemagne if he were to go back to France, he would follow him and be his loyal servant. However, the Saracen king only intended for Charlemagne and his men to go home. He had no intention of following.

Ganelon's Wicked Plan

1. **Who was sent as messenger to the Saracen king?**

   Ganelon was sent as the messenger to the Saracen king.

2. **Who suggested that Ganelon be sent?**

   Roland suggested Ganelon be sent.

3. **What wicked plan did Ganelon make?**

   Ganelon told the Saracen king that it was Roland who was causing the trouble. Ganelon informed the king that Roland would be in the rear ranks, and once Charlemagne was gone, they could attack Roland.

The Rear Guard

1. **Why did Roland ask to be given command of the rear guard?**

   Roland was given command of the rear guard because he was brave and liked to be where there was the most danger.

2. **Why did not Roland blow his horn for help when he first saw the enemy?**

   Roland did not blow his horn at first because he thought they could overtake the enemy.

Roland's Last Battle
Tell the story of Roland's last Battle.

> Four times Roland and his men were able to drive back the enemy, but they soon tired. Roland was sad to see so many of his men dead. He finally called Charlemagne to help so that no more men would be lost. When the Saracens realized that Charlemagne was coming to Roland's rescue, they all threw swords at Roland. Roland was injured to the point of death.

Make an outline for the story, using the subtitles as topics. Then choose seven of your classmates and, thinking of them as "minstrels", listen while they tell the complete story. (Formal outlines use Roman numerals for main topics. If students are not comfortable using Roman numerals have them use Arabic numbers or letters of the alphabet.)

   I. Roland's Boyhood
  II. Charlemagne Finds Roland
 III. Roland's New Home
 IV. Charlemagne and Roland in Spain
  V. Ganelon's Wicked Plan
 VI. The Rear Guard
VII. Roland's Last Battle

Find in the glossary the meaning of: content, governor, lance, hasty, conquered, knight.

Find in the glossary the pronunciation of: Saragossa, Sutri, Charlemagne, Ganelon, Saracen, Marsilius.

Extended Activities:

For any or all of the three stories in "Part IV," have students choose from one of the following:

  1. Draw a seven-part cartoon. For each part illustrate the main idea.

  2. Make a book of the main characters in the story. Draw a picture of the character then write a caption telling the main characteristics of that character.

  3. Write about a time when they showed great courage and/or determination.

ROLAND, THE NOBLE KNIGHT, p. 257

For any or all of the three stories in "Part IV," choose from one of the following:

1. Draw a seven-part cartoon. For each part illustrate the main idea.
2. Make a book of the main characters in the story. Draw a picture of the character then write a caption telling the main characteristics of that character.
3. Write about a time when you showed great courage and/or determination.

_____

_____

_____

_____

_____

_____

_____

_____

_____

_____

_____

_____

_____

_____

_____

_____

_____

_____

_____

Story

Reader p. 221

Find in the glossary the meaning of:

minstrel_____

victorious_____

warriors_____

sentinel_____

Goths_____

foe_____

grasp_____

hilt_____

comrade_____

Reader p. 239

regain_____

smithy_____

Denmark_____

forge_____

weld_____

toil_____

anvil_____

weapons_____

Reader p. 257

content_____

governor_____

lance_____

hasty_____

conquered_____

knight_____

Pronounce:

Hrothgar, Grendel, Sigurd, Brunhild, Saragossa, Sutri, Charlemagne, Ganelon, Saracen, Marsilius.

PART V:
GREAT AMERICAN AUTHORS

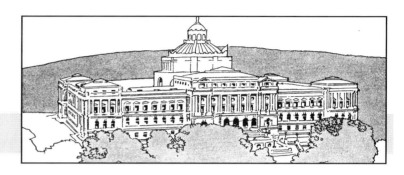

In This Section—

These stories and poems do not have "Helps to Study" questions in the reader. However, questions have been added in this teacher's guide to address those selections. These additional questions appear on separate worksheets which may be copied for the students.

** *The first number refers to the page in the reader on which the story begins; the second refers to the page in the "Helps to Study" section in the back of the student's reader in which the pertinent questions appear.*

† *See "Suggestions for Silent Reading" on page 3.*

Objectives—

By completing "Part V," the following objectives will be met.

1. The student will use effective reading strategies to construct meaning and identify purpose of text including:
   a. using illustrations
   b. defining unfamiliar words
   c. retelling and summarizing

2. The student will determine the main idea or essential message and identify relevant supporting details and facts of a text.

3. The student will read and organize facts from the text and other sources to make a report and outline and perform an authentic task.

4. The student will prepare for writing by focusing on the topic and organizing supporting details in a logical sequence.

5. The student will draft and revise writing in cursive.

6. The student will produce final documents that have been edited for correct spelling and punctuation.

7. The student will write for a variety of audiences and purposes.

8. The student will write in a variety of genres including narration, exposition, and poetry.

9. The student will use speaking strategies effectively such as using eye contact and gestures that engage the audience.

10. The student will be familiar with the common features of fiction and nonfiction.

11. The student will identify the development of plot and how conflicts are resolved in a story.

12. The student will identify and understand similarities and differences among the characters, settings, and events presented in various texts.

13. The student will identify and use literary terminology such as rhyme scheme and personification.

14. The student will respond critically to fiction, nonfiction, poetry, and drama.

15. The student will recognize cause-and-effect relationships in literary texts.

16. The student will respond to a text by explaining how the motives of the characters or events compare with those in his or her own life.

17. The student will understand the qualities necessary for people to become good citizens and apply those qualities to his/her personal life.

BENJAMIN FRANKLIN—

THE WHARF, p. 280*

1. **As a ten year old boy, Benjamin Franklin began work in his father's business. What was Benjamin's job?**

   He cut the wick for candles,
   took care of the shop, and ran errands for his father.

2. **Give two examples from this story that show Benjamin Franklin was "a leader among the boys."**

   When he and his friends ran into difficulty in their boats or canoes, Benjamin Franklin was "allowed to govern" in order to get them through the difficulty. He also led them into mischief when he got them to help build a wharf with someone else's stones.

3. **Read the sentence that describes the size of the stones they moved.**

   "In the evening, when the workmen were gone, I assembled a number of my playfellows, and working with them diligently, sometimes two or three to a stone, we brought them all away and built our little wharf."

4. **Benjamin Franklin's father convinced him "that nothing was useful which was not honest." With your classmates have a discussion about honesty by completing these starters: "Honesty is _____." "Honesty requires _____." Keep a record of your responses then decide whether Benjamin Franklin and his father would agree with your responses.**

Find in the glossary the meaning of: tallow-chandler, inclination, declared against it, bounded, quagmire, proposal, comrades, diligently, inquiry.

This selection does not have "Helps to Study" questions in the reader.

THE WHARF, p. 280

1. As a ten year old boy, Benjamin Franklin began work in his father's business. What was Benjamin's job?

    _____

    _____

2. Give two examples from this story that show Benjamin Franklin was "a leader among the boys."

    _____

    _____

    _____

3. Read the sentence that describes the size of the stones they moved.

    _____

    _____

    _____

4. Benjamin Franklin's father convinced him "that nothing was useful which was not honest." With your classmates have a discussion about honesty by completing these starters: "Honesty is _____." "Honesty requires _____." Keep a record of your responses then decide whether Benjamin Franklin and his father would agree with your responses.

PROVERBS FROM POOR RICHARD'S ALMANAC, p. 281

1. **Which of these proverbs seems most valuable to you?**
   Answers will vary.

2. **Notice that some of them teach thrift; what else do they teach?**
   They teach wise use of time and the value of hard work.

3. **Explain these proverbs in your own words.**
   Answers will vary.

4. **Tell what you know about Franklin's life. Franklin was also an inventor. He made a famous experiment that brought about the invention of lightning rods. How does the picture on page 279 (page 141 in *Teacher's Guide*) suggest this?**
   The picture shows lightning bolts in storm clouds with Franklin's picture in the center suggesting that he spent time experimenting with lightning.

Find in the glossary the meaning of: sluggards.

Extended Activity:

Have students create a time line of Benjamin Franklin's life, paying special attention to his inventions. For which inventions is he credited?

PROVERBS FROM POOR RICHARD'S ALMANAC, p. 281

Create a time line of Benjamin Franklin's life, paying special attention to his inventions.

For which inventions is he credited?

_____

_____

_____

_____

_____

A TRICK FOR DOING GOOD, p. 282

1. **Tell in your own words Franklin's "trick" for doing good.**

   When a friend asked Franklin for money, he gave it to him with the understanding that rather than to repay him, the friend would pass it on to someone else in need, who in turn would pass it on to others in need. The gift could, therefore, help many people.

2. **How could a "knave" spoil the plan?**

   According to your glossary, a knave is a " rascal" or a "cheat." A knave could spoil the plan by keeping the money that came to him, refusing to pass it on.

3. **Would the world be better if there were more such "tricks" for doing good?**

   Yes, the world would be a better place if everyone practiced more such "tricks."

4. **"Your most obedient servant"—an old way of ending letters.**

5. **What qualities had Franklin that helped to make him a good American citizen?**

   Franklin cared about the needs of others; he didn't hoard his money for himself, but shared it freely asking only that the kindness be passed along. He considered himself a servant to others.

Find in the glossary the meaning of: louis d'ors, enable, discharge, knave, cunning, prosperity.

Extended Activity:

Have students create a list of "random acts of kindness" they could do for others and then have students do them. Follow Franklin's advice that the kindness be passed on to someone else.

A Trick for Doing Good, p. 282

Create a list of "random acts of kindness" you could do for others and then do them. Follow Franklin's advice that the kindness be passed on to someone else.

_____

_____

_____

_____

_____

_____

_____

_____

John Greenleaf Whittier—

The Drovers, p. 284

1. **"There's life alone in," etc.—The only life worth living is, etc.**

2. **Do you find that satisfying "rest" comes only after you have been "striving"?**

   Answers will vary.

3. **Why does the poet call the drove "stately"?**

   In your glossary stately is defined as "dignified; serious looking and acting." The drove is stately since the cattle have traveled many miles and are slow and plodding as they travel along.

4. **With what does Whittier compare the horns of the cattle?**

   He compares the horns of the cattle to "plumes and crests," perhaps resembling the helmets of soldiers in battle.

5. **What picture do the seventh and eighth stanzas make you see?**

   Stanzas seven and eight describe a stampede when the cattle run wildly through a farmer's meadow until his family herds them back to the path again.

6. **What does the poet mean by the expression, "the baffled truants rally"?**

   The baffled truants are the confused cattle that rally or return to their stately march on the path.

7. **"Our charge"—the drove that is in our keeping.**

8. **What tells you that the drovers will start early the next morning?**

   "We'll go to meet the dawning, Ere yet the pines of Kearsarge Have seen the sun of morning."

9. **"The ears of home"—the ears of the wife and children.**

10. **Tell what you know about Whittier's life.**
    Answers will vary.

11. **What does the picture on page 283 (page 147 in *Teacher's Guide*) suggest?**
    The picture suggests Whittier knew about the hard work, "heat and cold, and shower and sun" that he wrote about in "The Droves." He grew up a farmer and understood their life well.

Find in the glossary the meaning of: striving, comrades, tavern, beechen, ample, plumes, crests, anon, pale, fallow, goodman, sally, Kearsarge.

THE FISHERMAN, p. 287

1. **Who is talking in this poem?**

   The title of the poem suggests the fisherman is talking.

2. **What do you see in the illustration on page 287 (right) that shows how "the breath of heaven" speeds the ship?**

   From the fullness of the sails and the height of the waves, one can see "the breath of heaven" or wind, speeds the ship.

3. **Change the order of the words in the first two lines of stanza three to make the sense clearer.**

   The steeple looks from the hill top and the lighthouse (looks) from the sand.

4. **"Change and chances of the ocean and the sky"—the risks due to sudden storms at sea.**

5. **To what does the poet compare the "scaly tribes" of fish?**

   The poet compares the "scaly tribes" of fish to a farmer's grain. Fisherman reap the "scaly tribes" as farmers reap their crops.

6. **"Working out our lot"—working faithfully on the task that is set before us.**

7. **"Whistle down the wild wind"—shout and sing and make merry.**

8. **"Freshening"—blowing stronger and stronger.**

9. **Why do the fishermen call the earth "dull"?**

   The fishermen consider life on land (the earth) dull next to the excitement of life on the seas where "We will whistle down the wild wind, And laugh beneath the cloud!"

Find in the glossary the meaning of: amain, heave, lubber, steed, teeming, congeals.

Extended Activities:

1. In the discussion sections of "Part III," "The Bee and the Flower," page 182 and "Raining," page 190 (pages 100 and 109, respectively, in the *Teacher's Guide*), students learned the definitions of alliteration and consonance. To reinforce that skill, have students read "The Fisherman" and list examples of alliteration and consonance.

seaward breezes sweep; Leave to the lubber landsmen; change and chances; From off the frozen reels; We will whistle down the wild wind; darkness as in daylight; beneath us is his hand.

2. Have students imagine that they want to live the life of the fishermen in this poem. Have them imagine, also, that they know nothing about sailing or fishing. Therefore, they must hire a crew that can manage their boats. Have students answer these questions: How will you select your crew? What skills will the crewmen need? What jobs and responsibilities will they have on board your boat? Appoint one student to lead your discussion, one to take notes, and another to present your conclusions to the class.

3. Stanza seven pictures the fishermen whistling while they work. Have students imagine themselves on their fishing boat conducting a song writing contest with the crew. Have students create the words to a song, using a tune they already know or creating an original tune to go with their lyrics.

THE FISHERMAN, p. 287

1. In the discussion sections of "Part III," "The Bee and the Flower," page 182 and "Raining," page 190 you learned the definitions of alliteration and consonance. To reinforce that skill, read "The Fisherman" and list examples of alliteration and consonance.

   _____

   _____

   _____

   _____

2. Imagine that you want to live the life of the fishermen in this poem. Imagine, also, that you know nothing about sailing or fishing. Therefore, you must hire a crew that can manage your boat. Answer these questions:

How will you select your crew?

   _____

   What skills will the crewmen need?

   _____

   What jobs and responsibilities will they have on board your boat?

   _____

   Appoint one student to lead your discussion, one to take notes, and another to present your conclusions to the class.

3. Stanza seven pictures the fishermen whistling while they work. Imagine yourself on your fishing boat conducting a song writing contest with the crew. Create the words to a song, using a tune you already know or creating an original tune to go with your lyrics.

   _____

   _____

   _____

   _____

THE FISH I DIDN'T CATCH, p. 289*

1. **When was the happiest moment in Whittier's life?**

   His happiest moment was when he received his first fishing pole from his uncle.

2. **What did Whittier catch on his first attempt?**

   He "brought up a bunch of weeds."

   Was he successful in later attempts?

   No, again and again he failed to catch anything. Finally he caught a pickerel, but it got away.

3. **How did his uncle encourage him?**

   He baited the hook and told Whittier to try again.

4. **In "Part II," "The Foolish Jackal" page 112 (page 62 in the *Teacher's Guide*), you were given several proverbs or morals—lessons about life—and asked to apply them to the story. In "The Fish I Didn't Catch" Whittier learns the moral "Never brag of your fish before you catch him." Here are several more. Explain how they relate to his fishing experience.**

   a) **Practice makes perfect.**

   b) **If at first you don't succeed, try, try again.**

   c) **Back to the drawing board.**

   d) **Don't cry over spilled milk.**

   e) **Easier said than done.**

   f) **Don't count your chickens before they are hatched.**

   g) **A miss is as good as a mile.**

Find in the glossary the meaning of: accompany, stroll, intensely, trudged, haunts, favorable, appealingly, gleam, hassock, shrewd, caution

This selection does not have "Helps to Study" questions in the reader.

THE FISH I DIDN'T CATCH, p. 289

1. When was the happiest moment in Whittier's life?

   _____

   _____

2. What did Whittier catch on his first attempt?

   _____

   _____

   _____

3. How did his uncle encourage him?

   _____

4. In "Part II," "The Foolish Jackal," you were given several proverbs or morals—lessons about life—and asked to apply them to the story. In "The Fish I Didn't Catch" Whittier learns the moral "Never brag of your fish before you catch him." Here are several more. Explain how they relate to his fishing experience.
   a) Practice makes perfect.

   _____

   _____

   b) If at first you don't succeed, try, try again.

   _____

   _____

   c) Back to the drawing board.

   _____

   _____

   d) Don't cry over spilled milk.

   _____

   _____

e) Easier said than done.

_____

_____

f) Don't count your chickens before they are hatched.

_____

_____

g) A miss is as good as a mile.

_____

_____

HENRY WADSWORTH LONGFELLOW—

DAYBREAK, P. 293*

1. **What does "Daybreak" describe?**
   It describes "the wind as it comes in from the sea at break of day."

2. **Personification is giving human qualities to non-human objects. What is personified throughout the poem?**
   The wind is personified.

Find in the glossary the meaning of: mariners, clarion, chanticleer, proclaim.

This selection does not have "Helps to Study" questions in the reader.

DAYBREAK, p. 293

1. What does "Daybreak" describe?

   _____

2. Personification is giving human qualities to non-human objects. What is personified throughout the poem?

   _____

   _____

Rain in Summer, p. 293

1. **Why does the poet call rain in summer "welcome"?**
   The rain is welcome because it comes after the "dust and heat" to cool things down.

2. **To what does he compare the plain, in the last stanza?**
   He compares the plain to a "leopard's tawny and spotted hide."

3. **On page 292 you read that Longfellow was a great lover of nature. How do the two poems you have just read prove the truth of this statement?**
   Longfellow's poems are about the weather and things found in nature. He presents them in a positive light.

4. **Tell what you know about Longfellow's life.**
   Answers will vary. Refer to page 292.

HIAWATHA'S FISHING, p. 295

1. The aim of an Indian boy was to be brave and strong, a great hunter, fisher, and warrior. How does this help explain why Hiawatha was so happy as he went "all alone" to catch the sturgeon?

   Hiawatha wanted to show how brave and strong he was.

2. **To what is the perch compared? The crawfish?**

   The perch was compared to a "sunbeam in the water" and the crawfish was "like a spider on the bottom."

3. **What fish was the first to take the bait? The second?**

   The first fish to take the bait was the perch and the second was the sunfish.

4. **How did the sturgeon prove his great size and strength?**

   The sturgeon proved his size and strength by swallowing up Hiawatha and his boat.

5. **How did Hiawatha overcome the sturgeon?**

   He smote the heart of the sturgeon.

6. **Notice that this story has two parts; what are the subtitles?**

   "The Pike and the Sun-Fish" and "Nahma, The Sturgeon" are the subtitles.

7. **Read the poem aloud to show how musical it is.**

Find in the glossary the meaning of: Gitche Gumee, transparent, exulting, erected, azure, winnowed, sable, summit, clamor, eddies, smote.

Find in the glossary the pronunciation of: Nahma, Hiawatha, Mishe Nahma, Shawgashee, Adjidaumo, Kenozha, Maskenozha, Ugudwash.

NATHANIEL HAWTHORNE—

THE SUNKEN TREASURE,

P. 303†

The Unsuccessful Voyage

1. **Describe Sir William Phips as he sat in Grandfather's chair after the king had appointed him Governor of Massachusetts.**

   He had a "strong and sturdy" frame. His face was "roughened by Northern tempests." His coat was embroidered with foliage and his waistcoat was flowered over with gold.

2. **Tell of Phips's early life.**

   He was a poor shepherd in Maine then went to work as a carpenter building ships.

3. **What promise did he make his wife?**

   He promised "Sometime or other, he should be very rich and would build a 'fair brick' house in the Green Lane of Boston."

4. **What news did he hear of the lost Spanish treasure ship?**

   She was 50 years sunk and no one had gone to find her.

5. **What did he decide to do?**

   He asked King James to send him to find the sunken ship.

6. **Tell the story of the Rose Algier's unsuccessful voyage.**

   They could not find the ship and the men tried to revolt. They returned to England.

7. **Why was Phips eager to make a second voyage?**

   He was eager to go on a second voyage because before he returned to England, an old Spaniard gave him directions to the ship.

Phips Finds the Treasure

1. **Who fitted out Phips with another ship?**

   Noblemen fitted out Phips with another ship.

2. **Why did he build a boat?**

   He built a boat so that he could get closer to the reef of rocks.

3. **Tell how the treasure was found.**

   An Indian diver went down to fetch a sea shrub and found the treasure.

4. **What became of the treasure?**

   The noblemen took most of it.

5. **What good qualities did Sir William Phips have that gave him confidence in himself?**

   He was diligent and did not give up finding the treasure. He was also true to his word by returning to England with the treasure.

6. **With the help of a classmate, tell the story of the sunken treasure, one telling about "The Unsuccessful Voyage" and the other about "Phips Finds the Treasure."**

7. **Tell what you know about Hawthorne's life.**

   Answers will vary. Refer to page 302.

Find in the glossary the meaning of: adorn, tufted, foliage, adz, waistcoat, province, laden, resolved, plundering, prospect, mutiny.

Find in the glossary the pronunciation of: Porto de la Plata.

THE MIRACULOUS PITCHER, P. 310†

Baucis and Philemon

1. **What kind of old persons were Baucis and Philemon?**

   They were "the kindest old people in the world."

2. **What kind of people were the villagers?**

   They were "selfish and hard-hearted."

The Two Travelers

1. **What kind of persons were the travelers?**

   They were dressed in an odd way, but cheerful.

2. **How did Baucis and Philemon welcome the strangers?**

   They invited them into their home and fed them.

The Marvelous Staff

1. **What was peculiar about the traveler's staff?**

   The staff had wings near the top and snakes were carved into the wood. The snakes looked like they were moving.

2. **What made Philemon think the traveler was an unusual person?**

   The stranger's feet sometimes rose from the ground.

3. **What names did the strangers have?**

   Their names were Quicksilver and Thunder.

The Wonderful Supper

1. **What was wonderful about the supper that Baucis and Philemon gave the travelers?**

   The pitcher of milk kept refilling itself and was never empty. The bread tasted fresh and the honey shone brightly.

The Punishment of the Villagers

1. **How did the traveler account for the mystery?**
    He said if he believed in such things, he would think the staff bewitched.

2. **What punishment came to the neighbors?**
    The neighbors were turned into fish and swam in the lake that covered the village.

3. **Why did the strangers say there was neither use nor beauty in such a life as that led by the villagers?**
    The villagers had no beauty because they were not hospitable.

The Reward of Baucis and Philemon

1. **What reward came to Baucis and Philemon?**
    They were granted one wish and their house was turned into a palace of white marble.

2. **How did the oak tree and the linden tree fitly represent the loving service of Baucis and Philemon?**
    The trees offered shade to any who passed by.

Discussion.   What lesson does this story teach?   Make an outline for the story, using the subtitles as topics: then choose seven classmates to tell the story, following these topics.

Phrases to Know:
*   **"bore no traces, " page 311, showed no signs**
*   **"sympathies of their nature," page 316, kindness they should have**
*   **"save when," page 317, except when**
*   **"how the case was," page 320, the state of affairs (the pitcher was empty)**
*   **"ceased to have existence," page 324, was now gone**

Find in the glossary the meaning of: Providence, clad, inquiry, repose, draught, curmudgeon.

Find in the glossary the pronunciation of: Baucis, Philemon.

Extended Activities:

1. Many of the stories in *Book Four* have a moral or lesson we can learn. Have students choose one of the morals from the book and write a story demonstrating the moral. Students should plan their work, write a draft, revise and edit before writing a final draft. Final drafts should be written in cursive.

2. Have students choose their favorite poem from *Book Four* and illustrate it.

THE MIRACULOUS PITCHER, p. 310

1. Many of the stories in *Book Four* have a moral or lesson we can learn. Choose one of the morals from the book and write a story demonstrating the moral. Plan your work, write a draft (below), revise and edit before writing a final draft. Final drafts should be written in cursive.

_____

_____

_____

_____

_____

_____

_____

_____

_____

_____

_____

_____

_____

_____

_____

_____

_____

_____

_____

_____

2. Choose your favorite poem from *Book Four* and illustrate it.

Story	Find in the glossary the meaning of:
Reader p. 280	**tallow-chandler**_____
	inclination_____
	declared against it_____
	bounded_____
	quagmire_____
	proposal_____
	comrades_____
	diligently_____
	inquiry_____
Reader p. 281	**sluggards**_____
Reader p. 282	**louis d'ors**_____
	enable_____
	discharge_____
	knave_____
	cunning_____
	prosperity_____
Reader p. 284	**striving**_____
	tavern_____
	beechen_____
	ample_____
	plumes_____
	crests_____
	anon_____
	pale_____
	fallow_____
	goodman_____
	sally_____
	Kearsarge_____
Reader p. 287	**amain**_____
	heave_____
	lubber_____
	steed_____
	teeming_____
	congeals_____
Reader p. 289	**accompany**_____
	stroll_____
	intensely_____
	trudged_____
	haunts_____

favorable

appealingly

gleam

hassock

shrewd

caution

Reader p. 293 mariners

clarion

chanticleer

proclaim

Reader p. 295 Gitchee Gumee

transparent

exulting

erected

azure

winnowed

sable

summit

clamor

eddies

smote

Reader p. 303 adorn

tufted

foliage

adz

waistcoat

province

laden

resolved

plundering

prospect

mutiny

Reader p. 310 Providence

clad

inquiry

repose

draught

curmudgeon

Pronounce:
Nahma, Hiawatha, Mishe Nahma, Shawgashee, Adjidaumo,
Kenozha, Maskenozha, Ugudwash, Porto de la Plata, Baucis,
Philemon.

APPENDIX

A BRIEF DESCRIPTION OF WORLD WAR ONE
BY ANDY JAMESON

World War One (also known as the Great War) lasted for four years—from 1914 to the end of 1918. The war was fought between Germany and its allies

World War One had ended just a few years before the original *Elson Readers* appeared. This event was fresh in the mind of Americans and profoundly changed the way they looked at themelves and their role in the world. This changed outlook is reflected in *The Elson Readers,* in both the literature that was included and in the study questions. This brief description of that great event is provided as both a source of background information and a starting point for parents, teachers, and students to begin discussions on this turning point in American history.

(Austria-Hungary of the Hapsburg Empire and Turkey of the Ottoman Empire) known as the Central Powers (or the Triple Alliance), and Great Britain, France, Russia, Italy, Japan, and, from 1917, the United States called the Allies. Germany was forced to fight the war on two fronts: the Western Front against the Allies and the Eastern Front against Russia. It was the first international conflict in which the United States participated.

The leading causes of the war were the alliance system of the late nineteenth century, which divided European states into two contending camps; the German victory over France in the Franco-German War (1870-71); the unification of Germany under Chancellor Otto von Bismarck and its rapid industrialization; the nationalist and ethnic agitation in the Balkans; and the fact that by 1900, European states were engaged in an escalating arms race and building vast military and naval forces in peacetime. The alliance system was symptomatic of the tension in European society between the growth of an international economy—the competition for goods and markets—and the political outlook of European states based on their own narrow national interests.

Bismarck set out to build a German empire based on the nationalistic premise that Germany also deserved a "place in the sun"—which meant an international political, economic, and military position like that of the British Empire. In Europe, the Germans claimed that they were being encircled by France and Russia. The entrance of Germany into the world scene exacerbated the intense rivalry for power and colonial markets in Africa, the Near East, and the Far East, as well as control of the seas. When the Germans decided to build a navy in 1891, they began the Anglo-German naval race.

The "race for empire" led to crises in Morocco, where Germany sent a gunboat to protect German interests, and in the Balkans, where Germany supported its Austrian ally against the national liberation movements which threatened the integrity of the Austro-Hungarian Empire. The three Balkan Wars (1912-1913), which were a prelude to World War One, also involved the Turks, whose Ottoman Empire had been disintegrating under the liberation movements of the Greeks and the southern Slavic peoples (Serbs, Croats, Bulgarians), and the Russians, who intervened in the Balkans as the "big Slavic" protectors of the Orthodox Christians—thus posing a threat to the Central Powers.

It was the nationalist movements in the Balkans which provided the "spark" that began World War One. On June 29, 1914, the heir to the Hapsburg Empire, Archduke Franz Ferdinand, was assassinated in Sarajevo (the capital of Bosnia). The Germans supported their Austrian ally, while the French supported the Russians. Protected by their navy, the British tried to maintain their policy of "splendid isolation," but the threat to the British naval forces in the North Sea from the German fleet, and with the French coast of the Channel open to German naval attack, the British were forced to protect their sea lanes and defend their French ally. When the Russians refused a German demand to stop their mobilization on the eastern border, Germany declared war (August 1, 1914), and France followed with its declaration (August 3). And when the Germans launched their Schlieffen Plan—a military strategy which involved a rapid thrust through Belgium to crush the French forces (in violation of the treaty which guaranteed the neutrality of Belgium)—Great Britain also declared war on Germany (August 4).

To supply their Russian ally, the British and French launched a disastrous naval attack on Turkey via the Dardanelles (1915), but the campaign was called off when the Allies lost 143,000 killed or wounded in the Gallipoli campaign.

169

On the Eastern Front, the early Russian offensive of 1914, which had driven into German territories in Prussia, Poland, and Galicia, was stopped and driven back by the Austro-German offensive of 1915.

By 1916, the war of maneuver on the Western Front ground to a halt, and it became a war of position and attrition—the massive armies were deadlocked in trench warfare. The machine gun—a new weapon—immobilized the troops which could advance only with staggering losses, while the tank, which was to become the antidote to the machine gun, and the airplane, the future antidote to the tank, were still in the experimental stages of development as weapons of war. The stalemate on the Western Front, however, ended when the Russians withdrew from, and the Americans entered, the war. The imperial Russian armies, plagued by poor military leadership and inadequate supplies, collapsed, and Czar Nicholas II was forced to abdicate from the internal pressure of the socialists (Marxists), especially from the leader of the Bolsheviks, the extreme faction of the Russian Marxists, V. I. Lenin (who formed the Communist party). When the czar abdicated, Lenin seized power in November, 1917, and the Bolsheviks signed the treaty of Brest-Litovsk with the Germans (December 3, 1917). At this point the war shifted to the Western Front, where the German High Command, under its Generals Hindenburg and Ludendorff, planned an offensive against the Allies. The Germans moved their army from the Russian front to the west via the railroad.

The German policy of unrestricted submarine warfare led United States President Woodrow Wilson to break off diplomatic relations with Germany, and when the British ship Lusitania was sunk with American passengers on board, and American ships were lost to U-boat action, he asked Congress for a declaration of war "to make the world safe for democracy,"(April 2, 1917). But it would be one year before the American military force and industrial production were prepared for war, and American soldiers arrived on the Western Front. With conscription administered by a Selective Service system, the armed services built a force of over four million. The government undertook the massive task of converting producers in the lumber, steel, automobile, and other industries to war production. Shipping tonnage increased from one million to ten million tons. The war effort encouraged citizens to conserve food (sugar was rationed and meatless Tuesdays were introduced) and fuel (daylight-saving time was adopted to save coal), and to purchase government Liberty bonds—the Treasury Department staged rallies at which Hollywood stars appeared to promote bond sales. At the same time, farmers were induced to grow more crops, and the production of civilian goods was cut (75,000 tons of tin were diverted to military production from children's toys and 8,000 tons of steel from the manufacture of women's corsets to munitions). The United States also provided loans to the Allies, which they used to purchase food and supplies.

While American military and economic power were geared up, the French and British suffered great losses in holding the line on the Western Front. When asked about an allied offensive, French General Pétain said, "I am waiting for the Americans and the tanks." In June, 1918, American troops under the command of General John J. Pershing, engaged the Germans at the Battles of Château-Thierry, Belleau Wood, and the Argonne, as 250,000 Americans were landing in France each month. Faced with this allied buildup, the German command realized that Germany could not win the war, and the government of Kaiser Wilhelm II began peace negotiations. By the time the armistice was signed (November 11, 1918), there were two million American soldiers in France and another million were heading for Europe. The Allies suffered ten million killed and twenty million casualties in the war, and the United States lost 115,000 dead and 315,000 casualties. While the allied losses far surpassed those of the Americans, it was the specter and the reality of American military and economic power that were decisive in ending the war.

In military history, World War One is notable for the brutal conditions under which the war was fought and for the incompetent leadership of the commanders—and the effect on the morale and discipline of the troops. The idea that soldiers were "manipulated from above" subject to the traditional military concept of obedience based on punishment resulted in revision of the military code of conduct.

Among the legacies of the war, which affected the course of the twentieth century, were the creation of the League of Nations (an international consortium), the rise of totalitarianism, and the imperial partition of the Near East (which resulted in the future states of Iraq, Syria, and Jordan).

GLOSSARY

a as in m<u>a</u>t   ə as in b<u>a</u>nana   ä as in f<u>a</u>ther   ∅ as in s<u>i</u>de
e as in b<u>e</u>d   ər as in f<u>urther</u>   aů as in l<u>ou</u>d   ŋ as in si<u>ng</u>
i as in t<u>i</u>p   ā as in d<u>ay</u>   ē as in n<u>ee</u>d   ō as in sn<u>ow</u>
ȯ as in s<u>aw</u>   ȯi as in c<u>oi</u>n   ü as in r<u>u</u>le   ů as in p<u>ull</u>
    ᵊ as in eat<u>en</u>   <u>th</u> as in hea<u>the</u>r

A

a bun dance (ə-'bun-dənts) plenty

a bun dant (ə-'bun-dənt) plentiful

ac ci den tal ly ('ak-sə-'dent-lē) by chance

ac com pa ny (a-'kəmp-nē) go with

ac cord (ə-'kȯrd) wish

ac cord ing ly (ə-'kȯr-diŋ-lē) there upon

ac cuse (ə-'kyüz) to blame

a chieve ments (ə-'chēv-mənts) the great things you have done

ac quaint ed (ə-'kwān-təd) on friendly terms

ac quired (ə-'kw∅rd) obtained; got

Ad ji dau mo (äd-ji-'dȯ-mō)

ad mit tance (əd-'mi-tənts) permission to pay a visit to

a dopt ed (ə-'däp-təd) taken as a son

a dorn (ə-'dȯrn) to make beautiful

ad vance (əd-'vants) march forward; advantages; benefits; opportunities

ad vent ure (əd-'ven-chər) an interesting experience, or happening

adz ('adz) a cutting tool used to trim off the surface of wood

af ford ed (ə-'fōr-dəd) gave

a glow (ə-'glō) rosy with happiness

a gue ('ā-gyü) fever and chills

a lert (ə-'lərt) ready; listening

a main (ə-'mān) with full force

a maz ing (ə-'mā-ziŋ) surprising

am ber ('am-bər) yellow

am mu ni tion (am-yə-'ni-shən) powder and balls

am ple ('am-pəl) large

an cient ('ān-shənt) olden

a nem o ne (ə-'ne-mə-nē) an early spring flower

171

a non (ə-ˈnän) and then at another time

an tics (ˈan-tiks) tricks

Ant werp (ˈan-twərp) a city in northern Belgium

an vil (ˈan-vəl) a block of iron on which metal is hammered into different shapes

anx ious (ˈank-shəs) worried

ap peal ing ly (ə-ˈpē-liŋ-lē) with a look that seems to beg for aid

ap pren ticed (ə-ˈpren-təst) agreed to give his services for a definite time in order to learn the trade

ap proach (ə-ˈprōch) draw near

ap prov al (ə-ˈprü-vəl) agreement

ar bor (ˈär-bər) a shelter of vines woven together

Ar gonne (ˈär-gän) a district in the northeast of France where the American soldiers did much hard fighting during the First World War

ar gu ment (ˈär-gyü-mənt) dispute

a rouse (ə-ˈrauz) alarm; frighten

ar tic les (ˈär-ti-kəls) various things

ar til ler y (är-ˈti-lər-ē) a part of the army that fights with cannon

as cend ed (ə-ˈsen-dəd) went up

as pect (ˈas-pekt) appearance

as sem bled (ə-ˈsem-bəld) collected

as sem bling (ə-ˈsem-bliŋ) coming together

as sur ance (ə-ˈshür-ənts) statement

a stir (ə-ˈstər) in motion

as ton ish ment (ə-ˈstä-nish-mənt) wonder; surprise

a stride (ə-ˈstrȯd) astraddle

a thirst (ə-ˈthərst) thirsty

ath let ic (ath-ˈle-tik) active; well built

at tached (ə-ˈtacht) very fond of

at tend ed (ə-ˈten-dəd) went to

at trac tion (ə-ˈtrak-shən) charm

Au gus tin (ȯ-ˈgəs-tin)

au to bi og ra phy (ȯ-tə-bȯ-ˈäg-rə-fē) story of one's life written by oneself

av er age (ˈa-vrij) ordinary

a ware of (ə-ˈwār) led to understand

az ure (ˈa-zhər) sky-blue

B

back ground (ˈbak-graund) back out of sight

bade (ˈbād) commanded

baf fled tru ants ral ly ('ba-fəld; 'trü-ənts; 'ra-lē) ones that ran away are collected and brought back

bail ('bāl) dip; scoop out

bait ed ('bā-ted) attracted

balm ('bälm) a sweet-smelling plant or tree

bark ('bärk) a small sailing-vessel

bat tal ion (bət-'tāl-yən) a body of foot-soldiers

Bau cis ('bȯ-kəs)

beam ('bēm) a large plank

beech en ('bē-chən) made of beech-logs

be held (bi-'held) saw

be hold (bi-'hōld) pay attention to

Be o wulf ('bā-ə-wülf)

be wil dered (bi-'wil-dərd) puzzled

be witched (bi-'wicht) enchanted

bil lows ('bi-lōz) ocean-like waves

Bjorn son, Bjorn stjerne ('byərn-sən; 'byərn-stərn)

blast ('blast) gust

bliss ('blis) happiness

blithe ('blØ<u>th</u>) joyous

bluff ('bləf) rough

Boones bor ough ('bünz-bər-ō) a settlement founded by Boone

bound ed ('baůn-dəd) ran rapidly with sudden leaps; bordered

bow er ('baů-ər) its leafy home

brac y ('brās-ē) refreshing

brah man ('brä-mən) a native of Hindustan who belongs to the highest class

brav ing ('brā-viŋ) bearing bravely.

breast work ('brest-wərk) a protecting wall hastily put up

breath less ('breth-ləs) holding the breath because of eager interest

brew ('brü) prepare something for drinking

bric a brac ('bri-kə-brak) odd things used as ornaments

brin dle ('brin-dəl) having dark spots or streaks on yellowish-brown

brink ('brink) edge; bank

brisk ly ('brisk-lē) in a lively manner

brood ('brüd) the young of birds hatched at the same time

Bru in ('brü-ən) a common name, in stories, for the brown bear

Brun hild ('brün-hilt)

brush wood ('brəsh-wůd) small branches of trees

buc ca neer ing ('bə-kə-ni-riŋ) robbing

budg es ('bə-jəs) moves

bul lion ('bůl-yən) silver that has not been made into coins

C

ca na ry (kə-'ner-ē) a kind of grass fed to birds

cane brake ('kān-brāk) thick growth of canes, plants with long, stiff, hollow stems, common in the south

cap tiv i ty (kap-'tiv-ə-tē) imprisonment

cap tor ('kap-tər) one who holds another as prisoner

ca ress (kə-'res) a gentle touch

car ry log ('kar-ē-lȯg) a two-wheeled cart used for hauling logs

cas cade (kas-'kād) flow

cat kin ('kat-kən) the soft, furry flower of the willow and other trees

cau tion ('kȯ-shən) warning; advice

cau tious ly ('kȯ-shəs-lē) carefully, that is, trying hard to give the right answer

cav ern ('ka-vərn) a large cave

cease less ('sēs-les) never-ending

cen tu ry ('sen-chə-rē) one hundred years

chal lenged ('chal-ənjd) demanded that he fight

chal len ger ('chal-ən-jər) one who demands of another that he fight

chan nel ('cha-nəl) the deep part of a river where the main current flows

chan ti cleer ('chan-tə-klir) rooster

charge of powder ('chärj) enough powder to load a rifle

Char le magne ('shar-lə-mān)

charm the countryside by your singing delight the people for a long distance

cheep ('chēp) chirp

Cher Ami ('shar; ə-'mē) good friend

chis el ('chi-zəl) a sharp iron tool used in carving statues and figures

cir cum stanc es ('sər-kəm-stan-səz) conditions; happenings

clad ('klad) dressed

clam or ('kla-mər) noise; shouting

clam or ous ('kla-mər-əs) noisy

clar i on ('klar-ē-ən) trumpet

cleared ('klird) opened up by removing the trees

clear ing ('kli-riŋ) open space where the trees had been cut

clev er ('kle-vər) smart

cliffs ('klifs) high, steep rocks or banks

clus ter ing ('kləs-tər-iŋ) growing together in bunches, or clusters

co', boss come boss (used in calling cattle)

col o nists ('käl-ə-nists) settlers in a new country

col o ny ('käl-ə-nē) a settlement

com bined (kəm-'bind) together

com fort ed ('kəm-fər-təd) cheered

com man der in chief (ka-'man-dər; 'chēf) the officer of highest rank in the army

com mon ly ('käm-ən-lē) usually

com mu ni ty (kə-'myü-nə-tē) neighborhood

com pan ion ship (kəm-'pan-yən-ship) comradeship; friendship

com pa ny ('kəm-pə-nē) number of people

com pelled (kəm-'peld) forced

com plain of (kəm-plān) am finding fault with

com plet ed (kəm-'plē-təd) finished

com plete ly (kəm-'plēt-lē) entirely

com rade ('käm-rad) companion

con fi dence ('kän-fə-dənts) trust; a feeling of boldness

con fi dent ('kän-fə-dənt) sure

con fu sion (kən-'fyü-zhən) shame

con geal (kən-'jēl) freezes

con quered ('käŋ-kərd) overcome

con se quen ces ('kän-sə-kwent-səs) results; whatever may happen

con sid er (kən-'si-dər) think over carefully

con sid er a bly (kən-'si-dər-ə-blē) quite a bit

con sul ('kän-səl) an official appointed by a government to live in some foreign country to care for its citizens in that country

con tempt i ble (kən-'temp-tə-bəl) worthless

con tend ing (kən-'ten-diŋ) fighting

con tent (kən-'tent) satisfied

con tents ('kän-tents) all that was in it

con tin ued (kən-'tin-yüd) kept up

con ven ient (kən-'vēn-yənt) comfortable

con ver sa tion (kän-vər-'sā-shən) talk

con vinced (kən-'vinst) proved to me

cord ed ('kōr-dəd) put into pile of a certain size

Corn wal lis (korn-'wäl-is)

cor por al ('kȯr-pə-rəl) the first rank in the army above private

corps ('kȯr) the largest division of the American army

course ('kōrs) path

court ('kōrt) a royal palace

cow boy ('kaü-bȯi) a cattle herder on horseback

crag ('krag) a rough, steep rock

crazed ('krāzd) insane

cre at ed (krē-'ā-təd) made up

crest ('krest) a tuft of feathers upon the head of a bird

crev ice ('kre-vəs) crack; opening

crit i cal ('kri-ti-kəl) dangerous; when things were at the very worst
crook ('krůk) bend
crown ('kraůn) the very top
cruised ('krüzd) sailed back and forth between various points
cun ning ('kə-niŋ) clever
cu ri ous ('kyür-ē-əs) strange
cur mudg eon (kər-'mə-jən) a bad-tempered and stingy person
cur rent ('kər-ənt) the swiftest part of a stream

D

Danes ('dānz) people who lived in what is now Denmark, Norway, and Sweden
dark some ('därk-səm) dark; gloomy
dazed ('dāzd) so surprised and happy he could hardly understand
de cid ed ly (di-'sī-dəd-lē) firmly
decks ('deks) decorates
de clared against it (di-'klārd) would not give his consent
de fi ance (di-'fī-ənts) daring him
del i cate ('de-li-kət) dainty; easily broken
de li cious (di-'li-shəs) very pleasant; delightful; full of enjoyment
de liv er ing (di-'li-və-riŋ) giving out
dells ('delz) valleys
de nied (di-'nīd) refused
Den mark ('den-märk) a country in Europe
dense ('dents) thick
de part (de-'pärt) leave; go away
de ri sion (di-'ri-zhən) scorn
de sert ed (di-'zər-təd) left alone
de serve (di-'zərv) have a right to
des per ate ('des-pə-rət) in very great danger
de struc tion (di-'strək-shən) ruin; downfall
de ter mi na tion (di-tər-mə-'nā-shən) strong purpose
de ter mined (di-'tər-mənd) decided
dif fi cult ('di-fi-kəlt) hard; uncommon
dif fi cul ty ('di-fi-'kəl-tē) trouble
dil i gent ly ('di-lə-jənt-lē) busily; steadily
dim ('dim) not able to see clearly
di rec tion (də-'rek-shən) thing she had been told to do
di rect ly (də-'rekt-lē) at once
dis a gree (di-sə-'grē) have ideas that are not the same
dis ap point ment (di-sə-'pȯint-mənt) failure to get what he expected

dis charge (dis-'chärj) pay

dis cour aged (dis-'kər-ijd) cast down; ready to give up

dis cov er (dis-'kə-vər) find

dis mal ('diz-məl) gloomy; sad

dis played (di-'splād) set out so it can be seen

dis pute (di-'spyüt) quarrel

Dis tin guished Service Cross (di-'sting-gwisht) small bronze cross on a ribbon given to a soldier for a very brave act

dis turbed (di-'stərbd) troubled

di vine (də-'vØn) heavenly; holy

di vis ion (də-'vi-zhən) one of the large sections of the American army

dol ing ('dō-liŋ) giving out in small portions

dot (dät) tiny thing

draught (drȧft) drink

drear (drir) gloomy

dreary ('drir-ē) cloudy; dark

drowse ('draüz) light sleep

drowsily ('draü-zə-lē) sleepily

drudgery ('drəj-ər-ē) work that is hard and uninteresting

drums ('drəmz) squirts the milk into the tin pail and makes a sound like a drum beat

du cat ('də-kət) old coin, worth about $2.28 [1920]

dun (dən) brown

dusk y ('dəs-kē) dark

E

ed dies ('e-dēz) small whirlpools

el der bloom ('el-dər-blüm) the white or pink flowers of the elder

em bark (im-'bärk) set sail

em bers ('em-bərz) small pieces of coal burning slowly

em pha sis ('em-fə-səs) force

en a ble (i-'nā-bəl) make it possible for you

en am el (i-'na-məl) a smooth, glossy substance placed upon metal, glass, or pottery for ornament or protection

en deav or ing (in-'de-və-riŋ) trying

en gulf (in-'gəlf) blot out

en sign ('en-sən) an officer of low rank

ere ('er) before

e rect ed (i-'rek-təd) turned up

es ti mat ed ('es-təm-mā-təd) valued; judged to be worth

ev er ('e-vər) always
ex ceed ing ly (ik-'sē-diŋ-lē) very
ex cel lent ('ek-sə-lənt) of good quality
ex claimed (iks-'klāmd) cried out
ex cla ma tions (eks-klə-'mā-shənz) shouts
ex haus tion (ig-'zȯs-chən) weariness
ex pe ri ence (ik-'spir-ē-ənts) practice
ex plained (ik-'splānd) said in such a way as to make his act understood
ex plor a tions ('ek-splə-rā-shənz) trips made to examine the country
ex plor ing (ek-'splō-riŋ) examining thoroughly
ex qui site (ek-'skwi-zət) very pleasing
ex ult ing (ig-'zəl-tiŋ) very happy

F

fag ot ('fa-gət) stick
fal low ('fa-lō) plowed land that has not been planted
fa mil iar (fə-'mil-yər) tame
fare ('fār) get along; food
fared ('fārd) journeyed
fas ci nat ing ('fa-sən-ā-tiŋ) very interesting; charming
fa vor a ble ('fā-və-rə-bəl) likely to be successful
feat ('fēt) deed, act
felled ('feld) cut down
fer tile ('fər-təl) having rich soil
fi ber ('f∅-bər) sinew; muscle
film ('film) thin skin
Flan ders ('flan-dərz) a district of Belgium
flaw ('flȯ) crack or break
fleece ('flēs) coat of wool
flint y ('flin-tē) stony; hard
flit ted ('fli-təd) flew quickly
flo rin ('flȯr-in) old coin, worth about forty-eight cents
flushed ('fləsht) rosy from exercise
flut tered ('flə-tərd) flapped his wings without flying
foe ('fō) enemy
fo li age ('fō-lē-ij) leaves
fore fa thers ('fȯr-fä-<u>th</u>ərs) ancestors
for est er ('fȯr-ə-stər) man who takes care of a forest
fore told (fōr-'tōld) told before it happens
forge ('fōrj) place to heat iron so it can be hammered into any shape

for mer ('fòr-mər) earlier

for ti fied ('fòr-tə-fød) made strong

fos ter broth er ('fòs-tər-brə-thər) one brought up as a brother, though not related

foun dered ('faùn-dərd) made themselves lame by eating too much

frame ('frām) build; body

franc ('fraŋk) French coin worth about twenty cents in olden times

fresh et ('fre-shət) a flood

fret work ('fret-wərk) open-work

front ('frənt) the position nearest the enemy

fru gal ('frü-gəl) scanty; economical

fruit ful ('früt-fəl) bearing large harvests

fu el ('fyü-əl) something to burn

fu ry ('fyü-rē) rage; fierce anger

G

gales ('gālz) strong winds; storms

gal lant ('ga-lənt) very brave

gal le on ('gal-yən) large ship, used in the time of Columbus and after

game ('gām) animals which are hunted, for food or sport

Ga ne lon (ga-nəl-'ōn)

gar ri son ('gar-ə-sən) soldiers guarding a fort

gasped ('gaspt) caught her breath

gazed ('gāzd) looked long

ge loo ri (ge-'lü-ri) a kind of chipmunk

ges ture ('jes-chər) movement

gills ('gilz) breathing-organs of a fish

Gitch e Gum ee ('gi-chē; 'gü-mē) Indian name for Lake Superior, meaning Big-Sea-Water

gleam ('glēm) shine brightly

glee ('glē) joy; happiness

glen ('glen) small, narrow valley

glis ten ing ('gli-sə-niŋ) shining

gloom ('glüm) darkness

glo ried ('glō-rēd) glorious

glow ('glō) brightness

good ly ('gùd-lē) large

good man ('gùd-man) master of the house

Goths ('gäths) people who lived in Northern Germany long ago

gov er nor ('gə-və-nər) ruler

grace ('grās) beauty
grad u al ly ('gra-jə-wə-lē) little by little; slowly
gran dee (gran-'dē) nobleman
grant ('grant) allow as a favor
grasp ('grasp) hold
grat ed ('grā-təd) scraped
grat i tude ('gra-tə-tüd) thankfulness
graz ing ('grāz-ing) eating grass
greet ing ('grēt-iŋ) addressing with politeness and respect
Gren del ('gren-dəl)
grid i ron ('grid-∅-ərn) broiler
grief ('grēf) great sorrow
griev ous ('grē-vəs) cross
grim ('grim) stiff; stern-looking
guidon ('g∅-dän) a flag
gym na si um (jim-'nā-zē-əm) a place for exercising

H

hail ing ('hā-liŋ) calling to handicap something that hinders one's success
har dy ('här-dē) strong enough to bear hardships
har ness ('här-nəs) saddle, blanket, and everything worn by a horse
harsh (härsh) rough
has sock ('ha-sək) a tuft of grass
hast y ('hā-stē) quick to act
haugh ty ('hȯ-tē) proud
haunts ('hȯnts) favorite places
head quar ters ('hed-kwȯr-tərz) the place from which the work of the army is directed
heave ('hēv) lift up
heaved ('hēvd) rose and fell as if it was hard to breathe
hedg es ('hej-əz) a fence formed by bushes growing closely together
heed ing ('hēd-iŋ) paying attention to
heif er ('he-fər) young cow
herbs ('ərbz) plants whose stems are used for food or seasoning
here aft er (hir-'af-tər) after this
here with ('hir-with) with this
hew ing ('hyü-ing) cutting and shaping
Hi a wa tha ('hi-ə-'wȯ-thə)
hilt ('hilt) handle
Hirsch vog el ('hərsh-fō-gəl)

hitherto ('hi-thər-tü) before this time

hoar frost ('hōr-fròst) white frost

hob ('häb) a shelf on the side of an open fireplace, on which a pot or kettle may be kept warm

hob bled ('hä-bəld) limped

hold ('hōld) defend

home ly ('hōm-lē) common; everyday

hom ing ('hōm-iŋ) trained to return home from a distance

hos pi ta ble (hä-'spi-tə-bəl) kind; friendly

hos pi tal i ty ('hä-spi-tal-ə-tē) food and lodging given in a kind and friendly manner

host ess ('hōs-təs) a woman who is entertaining a guest, or guests

house hold ('haús-hōld) all those who live in the same house

house wife ('haús-wØf) a woman who manages a household

hov el ('hə-vəl) cottage

Hroth gar ('hròth-gar)

hud dled ('hə-dəld) crowded together

hues ('hyüz) bright colors

huge ('hyüj) very large

hum ble ('həm-bəl) lowly; those who act not vain or proud

hum bug ('həm-bəg) nonsense

hu mil i ty (hyü-'mi-lə-tē) meekness

hurled ('hərld) threw with great force

husks ('həsks) the outside covering of some grains, nuts, etc.

husk y ('həs-kē) hoarse

hut ('hət) a small house

I

i de al (i-'dēl) perfect example of

ill got ten (il-'gä-tᵊn) obtained by wrong means

il lus trat ed ('i-ləs-trāt-əd) made clear so that its meaning is easily seen

i mag ined (i-'ma-jənd) made-up

im i tat ing ('i-mə-tā-tiŋ) doing in the same manner

im pu dent ('im-pyü-dənt) bold

in ci dents ('in-sə-dents) happenings

in cli na tion (in-klə-'nā-shən) liking

in hab i tants (in-'ha-bə-tənts) those who live in any place; dwellers

in no cent ('i-nə-sənt) pure and simple

in quir y (in-'kwØr-ē) search, by asking here and there

in sist ed (in-'sis-təd) held firmly to my plan

in stant ('in-stənt) of this month

in tense ly (in-'tens-lē) deeply

in ter rupt ed (in-tə-'rəp-təd) broke in upon her talk

i ris ('∅-rəs) a plant having large, handsome flowers of many colors; sometimes called "the flag"

isles ('īlz) small islands

J

jack al ('ja-kəl) the wild dog of Europe, Asia, and Africa

Je han Daas ('ya-han; 'däs)

jest ing ('jes-tiŋ) joking

jour ney-cake ('jər-nē-kāk) a kind of bread made of cornmeal

judged ('jəjd) guessed

jus tice ('jəs-təs) fair treatment

K

Ka yoshk ('kā-òshk)

Kear sarge ('kər-särj; here, 'kē-är-särj for rhyme) a mountain in New Hampshire

keel son ('kēl-sən) a beam above the keel

Ken o zha (kən-'ō-zhə)

knave ('nāv) a rascal; a cheat

knight ('n∅t) a warrior of a special rank in olden times

knee ('nē) a piece of timber used to fasten the beams of a ship to her sides

L

lad en ('lā-dᵊn) loaded with fruit

La fa yette ('la-fē-yet) the French general who helped the Americans in the Revolutionary War

la ment ing (lə-'men-tiŋ) mourning

lance ('lans) a long pole with a sharp steel head, used as a weapon

land mark ('land-märk) any object which marks a place

la pel (lə-'pel) the fold of the front of a coat

laths ('laths) thin strips of wood nailed on a wall to hold the plaster

lea ('lē) meadow; pasture

league ('lēg) a measure of distance; in some countries three miles

ledge ('lej) shelf

leg ends ('le-jəndz) stories which have been handed down

lei sure ly ('lē-zhər-lē) slowly
like wise ('lῙk-wῙz) also
lilt ing ('lil-tiŋ) lively; gay
limb ('lim) leg
lin nets ('li-nəts) small singing-birds
list less ly ('list-ləs-lē) as if he did not care about anything
lit ter ('li-tər) group of young animals all the same age
locks ('läks) curls
lodg ing ('lä-jiŋ) a place to stay
loi ter ing ('lȯi-tə-riŋ) staying
loom ('lüm) machine for weaving threads into cloth
lot ('lät) fortune; what we can make of our lives
lou is d'ors (lü-ē-'dȯr) French coins, then worth over $4.00 each
low ing ('lō-iŋ) mooing
low ly ('lō-lē) humble
loy al ly ('lȯi-ə-lē) in a patriotic way
lub ber ('lə-bər) awkward; knowing nothing about a boat
Lub bock, Sir John ('ləb-ək)
lulled ('ləld) made sleepy
lu mi nous ('lü-mə-nəs) shining

M

ma gi cians (ma-'ji-shənz) those who perform wonderful tricks
mag nif i cent (mag-'ni-fə-sənt) wonderful; splendid
main ('mān) chief; principal
maize ('māz) Indian corn
man tles ('man təlz) dresses
mar gins ('mär-jənz) shores
mar i ners ('mār-ə-nərz) seamen
Mar sil i us (mär-'sil-ē-əs)
mar vel ous ('mär-vəl-əs) wonderful
Mas ke no zha (mas-kē-'nō-zhə)
Mas sa soit (mas-ə-'sȯit)
mas ter buil ders ('mas-tər-'bil-dərz) skillful carpenters
mas tered ('mas-tərd) conquered
match less ('mach-ləs) there is nothing like it
match lock ('mach-lȯk) old-fashioned gun
mate ('māt) wife
mead ow close ('me-dō-klōs) a grassy place that is fenced
mel o dy ('me-lō-dē) tune; song

mer cies ('mər-sēz) blessings
mi gnon ette ('min-yən-et) a very fragrant garden flower
milch ('milk) that gives milk
mink ('mink) a small animal valued for its soft, brown fur
min strel ('min-strəl) musician; storyteller
mi rac u lous (mə-'ra-kyə-ləs) able to do wonderful things
mirth ('mərth) joy; happiness
mis chie vous ('mis-chə-vəs) naughty
Mish e Nah ma (mish-ē-'na-ma)
Mish ook ('mish-yük)
mi ser ('mø-zər) very stingy person
mis sion ('mi-shən) service; task
moc ca sin ('mä-kə-sən) a kind of shoe, first worn by Indians
mod eled ('mä-dəld) shaped
mon ster ('män-stər) a huge creature of strange form
mor al ('mȯr-əl) meaning; lesson
mor sel ('mȯr-səl) bit; mouthful
mo tioned ('mō-shənd) waved
mount ed ('maȯnt-əd) climbed up
mus cu lar ('məs-kyə-lər) strong
mu se um (myū-'zē-əm) a place where a collection of curious or beautiful
   things is kept
mu ti nous ('myü-tə-nəs) refusing to obey orders
mu ti ny ('myü-tə-nē) refusal to obey
muz zle ('mə-zəl) nose and mouth, taken together, snout
myr i ad ('mir-ē-əd) countless
mys ter y ('mis-tə-rē) secret

N

Nah ma ('nä-mä)
neigh bor hood ('nā-bər-hüd) people living near together
nest lings ('nest-liŋz) young birds that have not left the nest
no bles ('nō-bəlz) men of high rank
nook ('nȯk) place hidden away
note ('nōt) see; notice
nought ('nȯt) nothing

O

O bi on ('ō-bē-ən)

ob scure (ȯb-'skyu̇r) humble
ob served (əb-'zərvd) said
oc ca sion (ə-'kā-zhən) time
oc ca sion al ly (ə-'kā-zhən-ə-lē) now and then
O ne on ta (ō-nē-'ȯn-ta)
op por tu ni ty (ȯ-pər-'tü-nə-tē) chance
op posed (ȯ-'pōzd) argued against
or gan ized ('ȯr-gə-nīzd) started
or na men tal (ȯr-nə-'men-təl) beautiful
out right (au̇t-rīt) aloud
out tow ers ('au̇t-tau̇-ərz) rises high above
out wit ted (au̇t-'wi-təd) beaten by cunning
o ver came (ō-vər-'kām) won a victory over; conquered
o ver whelm (ō-vər-'welm) to cover over completely

P

pac es ('pā-səz) steps
pag eant ('pa-jənt) a play
pale ('pāl) fence
pal ette ('pa-lət) plate on which a painter mixes his colors
pall ('pȧl) covering; cloak
par tic u lar (pər-'ti-kyə-lər) special
par tridge ('pär-trij) a game-bird
pass ('pas) a passageway through a mountainous country
Pa trasche (pa-'träsh)
peak ('pēk) the very top
peer ('pēr) look as far as you can
per plex i ty (pər-'plek-sə-tē) troubled wonder
per se ver ance (pər-se-'vē-rənts) power to stick to a thing
per sist ed (pər-'sis-təd) kept on trying
per sis tence (per-'sis-tənts) determination
per son age ('pərs-ən-ij) person
per suade (pər-'swād) make willing
pew ter ('pyü-tər) a white metal formerly much used instead of silver
Phi le mon (fi-'lē-mən)
pierc ing ('pir-siŋ) bitter
pi o neer ('pī-ə-nir) one who goes to live in a new country
pipe ('pīp) to play on a musical wind instrument, as a fife; to sing
pit e ous ('pi-tē-əs) begging for pity
plead ed ('plē-dəd) begged

plod ding ('pläd-iŋ) walking with much difficulty or trouble
plumes ('plümz) feathers waving
plum y ('plüm-ē) feathery
plun der ing ('plən-də-riŋ) robbing
point ('pȯint) particular place
pol len dust ('pä-lən-dəst) a fine, yellow powder in seed plants
por ce lain ('pōr-sə-lən) a kind of fine, white earthenware
por tal (pōr-təl) entrance; doorway
Por to de la Plat a ('pȯr-tō; de; lə; 'plä-tə)
post ('pōst) the place where a body of troops is stationed
pot ter ('pä-tər) one who makes earthenware or stoneware articles
pov er ty ('pä-ver-tē) lack of money
pow er ful ('pau̇-ər-fəl) strong
pres ence ('pre-zənts) company
pre served (prē-'zərvd) protected; saved; kept
pro ceed ed (prō-'sē-dəd) went on
pro claim (prō-'klām) shout out
pro ject ing (prə-'jek-tiŋ) sticking out
pro nounced (prə-'näunst) declared; said that he was
pro pos al (prə-'pō-zəl) suggestion
pros pect ('präs-spekt) chance
pros per i ty (präs-'sper-ə-tē) success; good fortune
pros per ous ('präs-pər-əs) happy
prov erbs ('prä-verbz) wise sayings
Prov i dence ('prä-və-dənts) God
prov ince ('präv-ints) colony
pro vis ions (prə-'vi-zhənz) food
pur ple ('pər-pəl) turn to a purple color, that is, ripen
pur sued (pər-'süd) chased

Q

quaff ing ('kwäf-iŋ) drinking
quag mire ('kwäg-mø̈r) a piece of soft, muddy ground
quail ('kwāl) the bobwhite
quaint ('kwānt) queer; old-fashioned
quake ('kwāk) shake; tremble
qual i ties ('kwä-lə-tēz) things which make up character
quar ters ('kwȯr-tərz) place of lodging for soldiers
quest ('kwest) search
quick ('kwik) living

Quick sil ver ('kwik-sil-vər) Mercury, the messenger of the gods
quiv er ing ('kwi-vər-iŋ) trembling
quoth (kwōth) said; spoke

R

ra di ance ('rā-dē-əns) brightness
raft ers ('raf-tərs) a beam that helps to support the roof of a house
ral ly ('ra-lē) collect in order
ranch ('ranch) a large tract of land, on which cattle, sheep, or horses are raised
range ('rānj) reach
ran som ('ran-səm) money paid for the release of a prisoner
ra tion ('ra-shən) a fixed share of food
ra vine (rə-'vēn) a long, deep hollow made by running water
read i ly ('re-də-lē) quickly; promptly
re al i ty (rē-'a-lə-tē) actual fact
realm ('relm) world
rear ('rir) behind them
reb els ('re-bəlz) people who are setting up a government of their own, and fighting those who ruled them before
rec og nize ('re-kəg-nØz) knew
rec ol lect (re-kə-'lekt) remember
re cov er y (re-'kə-vər-ē) getting well again
re cruit (ri-'krüt) new soldier
reef ('rēf) rocks or a stretch of sand near the surface of the water
reel ing ('rē-liŋ) whirling
re frain (ri-'frān) chorus
re fresh ing (ri-'fresh-iŋ) cool and pleasant to the taste
re gain (ri-'gān) win back
re gard eth (ri-'gär-dəth) takes care of
Re gin ('rē-gin)
re gion ('rē-jən) section of the country
reigned ('rānd) ruled
re joiced (ri-'jòist) were happy
re leased (ri-'lēst) set free
rel ish ('re-lish) enjoy
re mark a ble (ri-'mär-kə-bəl) wonderful; noted for
rem nant ('rem-nənt) remainder
re mote (re-'mōt) far away
re mot est (re-'mō-təst) faintest

rend ('rend) tear

re pay (re-'pā) to pay back

re port (ri-'pōrt) the sound of a gun

re pose (ri-'pōz) rest; quiet

rep re sents ('re-pri-zents) stands for

re quired (ri-'kwȯrd) needed

res i dence ('re-zə-dənts) home

re sist (re-'zist) try to get away

re solved (ri-'zälvd) determined

re spect (ri-'spekt) honor

rev o lu tion a ry (re-və-'lü-shə-ne-rē)

rheu ma tism ('rü-mə-ti-zəm) a disease of the joints

ri dic u lous (rə-'di-kyü-ləs) foolish

rifts ('rifts) openings

ri ot ers ('rȯ-ə-tərz) those who attack the property of others

rip ples ('ri-pəls) waves slightly

riv u let ('ri-vyə-lət) stream; brook

rod ('räd) 16½ feet

rogues ('rōgz) rascals

Ro land ('rō-lənd)

Roo se velt, The o dore ('rō-zə-velt; 'thē-ə-dōr)

roun ding up ('raȯn-diŋ) going out on horseback and driving in

roy al ('rȯi-əl) belonging to a king; fit for a palace

ruffed grouse ('rəft; 'graȯs) a gamebird; the male bird has a ruff or tuft of feathers on its neck

ru ins ('rü-inz) the remains of a building after it has been knocked to pieces

Rum pel stilt skin ('rum-pəl-'stilt-skin)

S

sa ble ('sā-bəl) black

Sah wah ('sä-wə)

sal ly ('sa-lē) rush

samp ('samp) porridge made of Indian corn coarsely ground and browned

sam pler ('sam-plər) a piece of fine needlework, used only to show the skill of the worker

Sar a cen ('sar-ə-sən)

Sa ra goss a (sa-rə-'gȯs-ə)

sas sa fras ('sa-sə-fras) the bark of the root of the sassafras tree; the sweet smelling oil made from it is used as a medicine and for flavoring

sa vo ry ('sā-və-rē) pleasant to the taste

scant y ('skan-tē) small

scathe less ('skāth-ləs) unharmed

score ('skōr) twenty

scowl ing ('skaů-liŋ) frowning

scrim mage ('skri-məj) fight

sear ('sir) dry; withered

sen ti nel ('sent-nəl) soldier appointed to guard a place

ser geant ('sär-jənt) the second rank in the army above private

set tlers ('set-lərz) people who go to live in a new region

sharp shoot er ('shärp-'shü-tər) one who is a very good shot

Shaw gash ee (shȯ-'gä-shē)

sheaf ('shēf) a bunch of the stalks of grain tied together

shel ter ('shel-tər) protection

Shi va ('shi-və)

shoots ('shüts) young and tender parts of the branches

shorn ('shȯrn) robbed

shrewd ('shrüd) wise

shut tle ('shə-təl) an instrument used to carry the thread in weaving

Si be ri an (sø-'bir-ē-ən) belonging to a place in Asiatic Russia

sid ing ('sø-diŋ) the lumber in the outside wall of a frame house

Si gurd ('si-gürt)

sim i lar ('si-mə-lər) of the same kind

sin gu lar ('siŋ-gyə-lər) very strange

sit u a tion (si-chü-'wā-shən) condition

six pence ('siks-pents) an English coin worth about twelve cents [1920]

skulk ('skəlk) to sneak away

sledg es ('slej-əz) sleds

slough ('slü) a place full of mud and water

slug gards ('slə-gərdz) lazy people

smithy ('smi-thē) the workshop of a Smith

smote ('smōt) struck

soar ('sōr) fly high

so, boss be quiet, bossy

sound ly ('saůnd-lē) thoroughly

spines ('spønz) pointed, stiff growths

spire ('spør) steeple

spir it ed ('spir-ə-təd) lively

spir its ('spir-əts) feelings; courage

Squan to ('skwän-tō)

stag gered ('sta-gərd) moved unsteadily; stumbled

stal wart ('stȯl-wərt) strong

start ed ('stàr-təd) roused

state ly ('stāt-lē) dignified; serious looking and acting

states man ('stāts-mən) a man skilled in the affairs of government

stead fast ly ('sted-fast-lē) firmly

steed ('stēd) a spirited horse

stock ('stäk) number

straight way ('strāt-wā) at once

strand ('strand) run aground

strewn ('strün) scattered

striv ing ('strØ-viŋ) working hard

stroll ('strōl) walk; ramble

stub ble ('stə-bəl) the stumps of a kind of grain left in the ground

stud ding ('stə-diŋ) one of the upright supports on which the laths are nailed in making a partition

stur dy ('stər-dē) strong; healthy

sub ject ('səb-jikt) one who promises to obey another

sub mit ted (səb-'mi-təd) gave up

suc cess (sək-'ses) getting what she wanted; result

sum mit ('sə-mət) highest point

sun flushed (sən; 'fləsht) reddened by the sun, that is, ripened

su pe ri or (sù-'pir-ē-ər) larger

sup ply ing (sə-'plØ-iŋ) serving

sur round ed (sə-'raund-əd) formed a line all around them

sur round ing (sə-'raun-diŋ) neighboring

sus pect ('sə-spekt) lay the blame on

Su tri ('sü-trē)

swag ger ing ('swa-gə-riŋ) walking around in a conceited manner

swarm ('swòrm) crowd; mass

sway ing ('swā-iŋ) moving back and forth

swerve ('swərv) turn

T

tal low-chand ler ('ta-lō-'chan-lər) one who makes candles from the fat of animals

tav ern ('ta-vərn) hotel

taw ny col ored ('tò-nē-kə-lərd) yellowish brown

teem ing ('tē-miŋ) filled with fish

tend ed ('ten-dəd) looked after

thick et ('thi-kət) thick growth of trees and shrubs

Tho reau (thə-'rō)

thresh old ('thre-shōld) piece of wood under a door

thril ling ('thri-liŋ) exciting

tim id ly ('ti-məd-lē) as if she were a little afraid

toil ('tȯi-əl) hard work

tol er a bly ('tä-lər-ə-blē) rather

tolled ('tōld) struck

tom a hawk ('tä-mə-hȯk) light war ax

tomb ('tüm) monument; grave

top ple ('tä-pəl) fall

tor tures ('tȯr-chərs) terrible suffering; tottering; moving unsteadily

tow er ('taủ-ər) very tall building

town meet ing ('taủn-'mē-tiŋ) gathering of all the men living in the town to carry on the business of the town

trace ('trās) follow the path of

trail ('trāl) track

tran quil ('tran-kwəl) quiet; calm

trans par ent (trans-'pār-ənt) clear

tread ('tred) step; walk

trea sure ('tre-zhər) riches

trench ers ('tren-cherz) plates

tri um phant ly (trø-'əm-fənt-lē) happily because she thought she was right

trudged ('trəjd) walked sturdily

tuft ed ('təf-təd) decorated

tur moil ('tər-mȯil) disturbance

twi light ('twø-løt) the time just before dark

U

U gud wash (ü-'güd-wȯsh)

um pire ('əm-pør) person chosen to settle a dispute

un com plain ing ly (ən-kəm-'plā-niŋ-lē) cheerfully

un der stand ing (ən-dər-'stan-diŋ) idea of the meaning

u ni verse ('yü-nə-vərs) world

un just (ən-'jəst) unfair

un tir ing (ən-'tø-riŋ) working all the time

urge ('ərj) persuade by repeating

ut ter ('ət-ər) tell; complete

V

vale ('vāl) little valley

va ri ous ('vār-ē-əs) different
vast ('vast) far-reaching
ven i son ('ve-nə-sən) deer meat
ven ture ('ven-shər) dare; do timidly; go safely
ven ture some ('ven-shər-səm) ready to run into danger
vi cious (vi-shəs) wicked
vic to ri ous (vik-'tō-rē-əs) successful
view ('vyü) sight
vig or ous ('vi-gə-rəs) healthy; full of life
viv id ly ('vi-vəd-lē) plainly; clearly
vowed ('vaůd) made a solemn promise to himself

W

wa ger ('wā-jər) prize
waist coat ('wāst-kōt) vest
wake ('wāk) track
Wal den ('wȯl-dən)
wares ('wārz) goods; articles
war i ly ('wār-ə-lē) carefully; as if afraid
war riors ('wȯr-yərz) fighting men
wa ver ('wā-vər) pause; sway from one side to the other
wax ing ('wak-siŋ) growing
way far er ('wā-fār-ər) traveler; person going along the road
weak ling ('wē-kliŋ) one who is not strong and healthy
weapons ('we-pənz) things to fight with
wear y (wē-rē) tired
weath er beat en ('we-t͟hər-bē-tən) worn and soiled from being out in all
    kinds of weather
weld ('weld) join by melting and hammering
well a day ('wel-ə-dā) alas
wick et ('wi-kət) gate
Wig laf ('wi-gləf)
wil der ness ('wil-dər-nəs) country not settled or cultivated
will ('wil) willingness
win nowed ('wi-nōd) moved as if separating grain from chaff
wist ful ('wist-fəl) sad; longing
with ered ('wi-t͟hərd) dried
with out (with-'aůt) out of doors
with stand (with-'stand) be strong; hold out against

wit ness ('wit-nəs) one who has seen or can prove a thing
wrap pers ('rap-ərs) outer garments
wrought ('ròt) made
wry ('rØ) crooked; as if he did not like the thought

Y

year ling ('yir-liŋ) an animal one year old
yield ed ('yēl-dəd) brought forth
yoke ('yōk) harness
yon ('yän) yonder; those

Z

zig zag ('zig-zag) crooked
zo o log i cal gar dens (zō-ə-'lä-ji-kəl; 'gär-dənz) public parks where animals, birds, etc., are kept

Books Available from
Lost Classics Book Company
American History

Stories of Great Americans for Little Americans..............................Edward Eggleston
A First Book in American History...Edward Eggleston
A History of the United States and Its People...................................Edward Eggleston

Biography

The Life of Kit Carson.. Edward Ellis

English Grammar

Primary Language Lessons...Emma Serl
Intermediate Language Lessons...Emma Serl

(Teacher's Guides available for each of these texts)

Elson Readers Series

Complete Set ....William Elson, Lura Runkel, Christine Keck
The Elson Readers: Primer...William Elson, Lura Runkel
The Elson Readers: Book One...William Elson, Lura Runkel
The Elson Readers: Book Two...William Elson, Lura Runkel
The Elson Readers: Book Three..William Elson
The Elson Readers: Book Four..William Elson
The Elson Readers: Book Five.......................................William Elson, Christine Keck
The Elson Readers: Book Six..William Elson, Christine Keck
The Elson Readers: Book Seven......................................William Elson, Christine Keck
The Elson Readers: Book Eight......................................William Elson, Christine Keck

(Teacher's Guides available for each reader in this series)

Historical Fiction

With Lee in Virginia...G. A. Henty
A Tale of the Western Plains...G. A. Henty
The Young Carthaginian..G. A. Henty
In the Heart of the Rockies..G. A. Henty
For the Temple..G. A. Henty
A Knight of the White Cross..G. A. Henty
The Minute Boys of Lexington...Edward Stratemeyer
The Minute Boys of Bunker Hill..Edward Stratemeyer
Hope and Have...Oliver Optic
Taken by the Enemy, First in *The Blue and the Gray Series*...............Oliver Optic
Within the Enemy's Lines, Second in *The Blue and the Gray Series*......Oliver Optic
On the Blockade, Third in *The Blue and the Gray Series*......................Oliver Optic
Stand by the Union, Fourth in *The Blue and the Gray Series*................Oliver Optic
Fighting for the Right, Fifth in *The Blue and the Gray Series*...............Oliver Optic
A Victorious Union, Sixth and Final in *The Blue and the Gray Series*......Oliver Optic
Mary of Plymouth...James Otis

For more information visit us at: http://www.lostclassicsbooks.com